This sequel to *Crime Buster* captivating as Carolyn Keene's iconic Nancy Drew series. Kiki's ability to personify cats as detectives is highly imaginative and engaging. Readers may actually forget the characters are animals—until they realize the cunning humor Kiki has slipped in. Revisiting Chim Chim, Simone, and the others as they grapple with very real "human" issues is guaranteed to please readers of all ages.

—**Thomas P. Gill,** author of *Maddy's Week at the Beach* children's series

Kiki Houser speaks two languages: human and cat. She captures the spirit, spunk, and sassiness of our feline heroine Chim Chim perfectly, allowing readers to step into the mind of a feline detective. Join Chim Chim, Simone, Zoe, and a whimsical network of fuzzy-faced friends as they work together to solve another mystery. Great for all ages, mystery lovers and animal enthusiasts alike.

—**Caitlynne Garland,** author of *River the Three Legged Dog*

Praise for *Crime Busters, Inc.: The Alligator Alibi*

Houser delivers a fun, rousing, action-filled story with abundant appeal to reluctant readers and animal lovers alike. The feline protagonists are amiable, tough, and quirky detectives, while the cast of usual suspects is anything but usual. Houser's own affection for animals—from furry to scaled—comes through the gentle, endearing writing and spot-on characterizations.

—**The BookLife Prize**

Ms. Houser does an excellent job of creating an entire neighborhood full of memorable animal characters. As an adult, I'm not embarrassed to say I'm looking forward to the next book in Kiki Houser's *Crime Busters, Inc.* series.

—**N.K. Wagner,** author of *Seascapes: poems for people who hate poetry*

Pet Poison No. 9

Kiki Houser

COMET
TALE
BOOKS

Published by Comet Tale Books—an imprint of Electric Moon Publishing, LLC

©2021 *Crime Busters, Inc.: Pet Poison No. 9* / Kiki Houser

Paperback ISBN: 978-1-955707-04-6
E-book ISBN: 978-1-955707-05-3

JUVENILE FICTION / Mysteries & Detective Stories
JUVENILE FICTION / Animals / Cats

Comet Tale Books / Electric Moon Publishing, LLC
P.O. Box 466
Stromsburg, NE 68666
info@emoonpublishing.com

Interior cat illustrations copyright © Scarlett Houser (2022)
Cover Design copyright © Cody Rayn & Lyn Rayn / Electric Moon Publishing Creative Services
Interior Design copyright © Lyn Rayn / Electric Moon Publishing Creative Services
Author photo copyright © Wendi Fuller Photography 2021

Library of Congress Cataloging-in-Publication data available. LCCN: 2022901168

Printed in the United States of America

An imprint of Electric Moon Publishing, LLC
www.emoonpublishing.com

For my mother, Dulcie Mae . . .
Though you didn't live to see your dream realized,
that dream lives on in me.

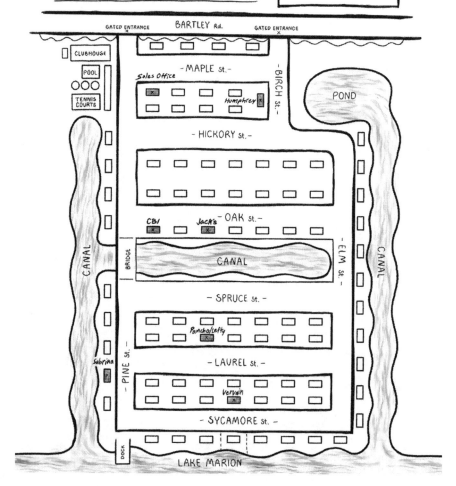

-HIGHLAND OAKS DEVELOPMENT-

RETAIL SHOPS

GATED ENTRANCE   BARTLEY Rd.   GATED ENTRANCE

CLUBHOUSE

POOL

TENNIS COURTS

- MAPLE St. -

Sales Office

Humphrey

- HICKORY St. -

- OAK St. -

CBI   Jack's

CANAL

BRIDGE

CANAL

BIRCH St. -

POND

ELM St. -

- SPRUCE St. -

Pancho/Lefty

- LAUREL St. -

Sabrina

- PINE St. -

Vervain

- SYCAMORE St. -

DOCK

LAKE MARION

Contents

CHAPTER 1
Flirting with Danger

The night was dark with no moon in sight. Chim Chim Tanner watched safely from the bushes, her sharp feline gaze fixed on the stranger who lounged on her doorstep. He seemed to laugh at her as he stared back with a wicked, one-toothed grin. The light behind his eyes called out both an invitation and a warning—almost a "come closer if you dare" look. She shuddered.

She stayed frozen, wondering if she should break cover and run. Suddenly an eerie cry broke the stillness of the night. "Chim Chim! Here, kitty, kitty!"

Chim Chim's eyes shifted slightly to the left of the jack-o-lantern. Her owner stood framed in the light of the doorway. Audrey cupped her hands around her mouth as she called out again. "*Ch-i-i-m* Chim!"

Relief flooded through Chim Chim. She left the safety of the bushes and sprinted across the street, keeping low to the ground. She fixed one eye warily on the stranger as she darted up the steps.

"There you are!" Audrey exclaimed. "You know I don't like you out at night in October. Halloween is only a couple of weeks away, and it's not safe for black cats."

"Hmph!" Chim Chim snorted as she slinked past Audrey's legs. *It's not safe for black cats in their own yards, either!*

She padded toward the kitchen, stopping to give herself a brief lick and remove all traces of her encounter—it wasn't dignified for a private detective to show fear. She joined Simone, her best buddy and partner at Crime Busters, Inc., as Audrey filled their food bowls.

"There you are," Simone said, cocking her white, furry head.

Didn't I just hear that line? Chim Chim thought, raising an eyebrow.

"Where've you been?" Simone prodded.

"Out scouting the night," Chim Chim said. "You know this is my *favorite* time of year."

"Yeah, but it's also the most dangerous time for a black cat," Simone reminded her.

"You sound like Audrey."

"Well, sometimes it takes *two* of us to keep an eye on you," Simone said with a grin.

Chim Chim shrugged.

"You'll never guess what I overheard earlier," Simone said, lowering her voice to a whisper.

Chim Chim swallowed a bite of food and stared at Simone impatiently.

"Audrey has started dating."

"Dating," Chim Chim repeated. Suddenly her mouth

dropped open. *"Dating?* As in . . . she has a boyfriend?"

"Yes!"

Chim Chim exhaled loudly. In all of her five years, she had no memory of Audrey *ever* dating. "Do we know anything about the guy?"

"Only that his name is Neal—Neal Schuler," Simone said. "She met him through a friend at work." She glanced over at their owner, who was stirring a pot on the stove. "I overheard her telling her sister about him on the phone. She said he works in insurance. She also said he's 'cute.'"

"Cute?" Chim Chim snorted. "All humans look alike, if you ask me." She finished her dinner, then lapped up a quick drink and started across the kitchen.

"There's one more thing," Simone said.

Chim Chim paused mid-step.

"Audrey acted very giddy when she talked about him. I've never seen her like this before. She smiled the whole time—with *all* her teeth showing!"

"*All* her teeth?" Chim Chim asked. "And she wasn't defending her territory?"

"Nope. She was completely alone."

"Hmm," Chim Chim murmured. Humans displayed such odd behavior. Whether she was five years of age or ten, she didn't think she would ever understand them.

She eyed the pet door, then changed her mind. She padded toward the open sliding glass door in the living room instead. Chim Chim stepped out into the Florida room—another name for a screened patio—and headed toward the glass-topped table. Leaping lightly onto its surface, she began her after-meal cleaning routine. Simone soon joined her.

"Any news of when Zoe might come home?" Chim Chim asked, pausing. Their feline housemate had fallen ill last week, and the vet seemed in no hurry to release her. Chim Chim hated to admit it, but she actually missed the grouchy old girl. Sure, there had been some friction between them when she was younger. But they had done a lot of feline bonding during the missing-pets investigation last year.

"No, I haven't heard Audrey mention it to anyone," Simone replied, "which is puzzling. Normally, she would have bitten off all her fingernails and called the vet's office ten times by now. I bet she's—"

They were interrupted by the bell-like ring of the telephone. Audrey appeared in the doorway, phone cradled against her ear. "Hi, Neal!" she exclaimed, grinning broadly.

Her teeth are *all showing!*

"Yes, it's good to hear *your* voice, too." Audrey grasped the handle on the sliding glass door and pulled it shut with a loud *thud*. Her voice was muffled as she disappeared from view.

Chim Chim turned to Simone with a raised brow. "What? Now she can't talk in front of us?"

Simone shrugged. "I—I don't know. This is all new territory for me."

Chim Chim sighed, shaking her head. She lay down, stretching her forepaws out before her—usually a relaxing position, but tonight she couldn't shake an odd feeling of unease. Was she still ruffled by the jack-o-lantern?

Possibly. It was silly to let such a trivial thing get to her. But even the best private detectives had a weak moment now and then. She was sure she would feel better tomorrow. She gave a convincing nod as a cool night breeze ruffled her fur and a lone frog chirruped in the darkness.

Chim Chim woke slowly, leisurely, from a most luxurious sleep. It was Saturday—a morning without the screeching sound of Audrey's alarm clock before the sun had even risen. It was also a morning without the chaos of Audrey hurrying to get ready for work. Chim Chim stretched and leaped off the bed, padding down the hall to the kitchen. She could hear birds singing outside and knew it was going to be a beautiful day, typical of Florida in October. The less humid air and slightly cooler temperatures made Chim Chim want to spend more time outdoors—something she avoided in the summer. The Florida sun showed no mercy for a cat with black fur!

She passed Audrey, who was singing in the kitchen and clanging about while making breakfast. Chim Chim paused, narrowing her eyes, then continued to the food bowls. She quickly swallowed the three or four kibbles at the bottom of her bowl and gave her owner a meow of protest. Audrey continued to cook, oblivious to her dismay. *This won't do,* Chim Chim thought. *I'll have to show her who's boss.* She uttered a higher-pitched meow that bordered on a wail, causing Audrey to stop mid-song and look down at her.

"Not now, Chim Chim," Audrey said, shooing her into the living room with a dish towel.

"Hmph!" Chim Chim snorted. She joined Simone on the couch. "What's the deal?" she asked, jerking her head toward the kitchen. "Audrey wouldn't get me any breakfast— *and* she swatted me with a towel, like a common animal!" She twisted her neck to lick the spot where the material had touched her fur. It was downright degrading!

"I don't know," Simone said. "But she's been doing a lot of that lately."

"A lot of what?"

"Singing—a little odd for Audrey, don't you think?"

"Definitely," Chim Chim agreed. "Especially in the morning. Do you think it has to do with her new *boyfriend?*" She drew out the last word.

"Possibly," Simone mused. "It's too early to tell."

"I bet she wouldn't treat Zoe so poorly," Chim Chim said.

"Probably not."

Simone didn't seem in the mood to talk, so Chim Chim turned her attention to the television.

Audrey appeared in the doorway, a reddish-brown strand of hair tucked behind each ear. "Okay, girls," she said. "I'm going to need you two to hang out in the bedroom for a while. I have a guest coming for breakfast, and I'm not sure how he feels about pets." She looked down at Chim Chim, her eyes narrowing. "Especially *bad* ones that get on the kitchen counters."

Chim Chim protested with a sharp whine as Audrey tucked her under one arm and then reached for Simone. "I know she's not—what the heck is she doing?" Chim Chim squeaked, unable to get a full breath. "I refuse to be manhandled—I mean, *womanhandled!*" She continued to struggle as Audrey carried them down the hall to the bedroom. Chim Chim was dropped abruptly onto the bed, followed by Simone. Then Audrey shut the door firmly behind her.

"Can you believe this?" Chim Chim asked. "Never in my years . . ." She trailed off.

"Nor in mine," Simone agreed, her brow furrowing.

The doorbell rang a few seconds later. They heard Audrey's quick footsteps in the front hall, followed by the sound of the door closing and a low muffle of human voices.

"She'll come to her senses in a minute," Chim Chim declared. "She'll *beg* our forgiveness for such rude behavior!"

Simone nodded slowly, as if she didn't believe her.

"Just watch."

They both stared at the bedroom door, waiting, until almost an hour had passed. Finally, Chim Chim lay down with a deep sigh and closed her eyes.

CHAPTER 2
Jack-in-a-box

By Monday morning, things were back to normal. Simone ate her breakfast in silence, pausing to study Audrey between bites. Their owner flitted around the kitchen in her usual morning rush. Except for her hint of a smile, there was no evidence of the recent change in Audrey's behavior. Simone shook her head.

Chim Chim swallowed a mouthful of food. "So . . . do we have any new Crime Busters business to take care of?" She glanced up as Audrey rushed past them on her way to the bathroom.

"No, but I wouldn't worry too much," Simone said. "It's actually nice to have a break, don't you think?" Their case log had been overflowing for several months, since they'd exposed the illegal activities of Divinity Laboratories last year. It had gained them local—well, local *animal*—attention.

"Yes, it certainly is," Chim Chim agreed with a grin. She started to stretch, then stopped, the grin quickly disappearing. "Still no news of Zoe?"

"No—and the whole thing's quite odd." Simone frowned.

"Odd how?" Chim Chim asked.

"Well . . . think about it. Zoe seemed perfectly healthy when she went in for her annual checkup last week, right? Then afterward, as you remember, she began throwing up everywhere. So Audrey took her back to Dr. Edwards's office, and she's been there ever since. I overheard Audrey saying they ran all kinds of tests but couldn't find anything wrong with her." Simone shook her head. "If you ask me, it must have something to do with that place. They must have done *something* there—either accidentally or knowingly—to make her so sick."

"Yeah, but if that's true, how could we prove it?" Chim Chim asked.

"I have no idea, little buddy. But the first step is getting her home, where she'll be safe."

Chim Chim nodded, falling silent.

Audrey dashed toward the door, pausing to look back at them. "Have a good day, girls!" She flashed them a smile, then exited to the garage. The door slammed shut behind her, immediately followed by the loud clanging of the metal garage door.

Simone knew their owner's morning routine. At least that much hadn't changed. She finished the last of her breakfast kibbles as the garage door closed with a noisy *clang, clang, clang!* Then she ran her tongue around the corners of her mouth. "I'm going out to clean up. You coming?"

"Of course."

Simone pushed through the pet door and out to the Florida room. She leaped onto the patio table and twisted her neck to begin a thorough lick of her right shoulder.

Chim Chim darted over and sprang, landing heavily on the glass-topped table. She cringed as the table wobbled slightly. "Sorry!"

Simone gave a sigh of annoyance as she waited for the table to steady. Then she went back to grooming.

Their baths were interrupted as a boxy white truck pulled up at the end of their sidewalk. The vehicle had a bright blue eagle and a red-and-blue stripe along its side.

"Mail delivery," Chim Chim observed.

A blond lady dressed in dark blue shorts and a pale blue shirt stepped down from the vehicle. Her shirt was adorned with a blue eagle that matched the image on the truck, and her long hair was pulled back in a ponytail. The lady reached in and pulled out a small box. She carried the package down the sidewalk toward them and laid it on the doorstep. Then she pressed the doorbell once and strode away. She climbed back into her vehicle and drove the short distance down Oak Street to the next mailbox.

Simone looked over at Chim Chim. She could tell her buddy was curious. The little cat's ears remained perked, and her gaze was locked on the screen door. Her tail swished back and forth in an agitated manner. "Want to see what it is?"

"I thought you'd never ask!" Chim Chim declared, leaping down from the table and sprinting to the outer pet door. She bolted through the flap with a *swoosh! Clang, clang, clang!*

Simone chuckled as she followed her housemate out to the sidewalk.

Chim Chim stood over the small box, squinting at the tiny postage label. "It's for Audrey."

"Of course it is—I almost got caught the last time I ordered something, remember? I won't be trying *that* again." Simone peered at the return address on the box's label. "Economy Pet Supply, Miami, Florida," she read. "Hmm. I wonder what it might be."

"Dunno." Chim Chim shrugged. "Doesn't matter—it's not for us."

"Well, technically it *is* for us, as we're the 'pets' in this household."

"True." Chim Chim turned as the clicking of toenails on pavement reached their ears. "Hey, it's Jack."

Simone looked up from the package. "Looks like Mr. Faulkner is taking him for his morning walk." A man wearing tan Bermuda shorts and a navy-blue Hawaiian-print shirt approached with a Jack Russell terrier on a leash. His white hair was covered with a floppy fishing-style hat. An unlit pipe hung from the corner of his mouth, the bowl resting against his trim white beard.

"Hey, Jack!" Chim Chim called out. She frowned as Jack walked silently by, seeming unaware of their presence. "Well, that's odd."

"Odd, indeed," Simone agreed. Something didn't seem quite right about their little friend. Jack's usual fast-paced, energetic gait had been replaced with a sluggish shuffle, like someone walking in their sleep. His eyes seemed focused on some distant point ahead of him, and his tail—usually wagging a mile a minute—was quite still. "*Jack!*" she called loudly as he passed the mailbox.

The terrier came to an abrupt stop, turning his head slowly in their direction. "Oh, hello . . . Simone," he said. His eyes seemed almost glazed, and they didn't focus on her at all.

"Jack, come on. What in blazes are you stopping for?" Mr. Faulkner sputtered through the dangling pipe. Simone knew Jack's owner could be quite grumpy since he'd quit smoking a year ago. She felt sorry for his little dog—and his wife.

Mr. Faulkner jostled the leash to get the terrier's attention. "Oh, sorry," Jack mumbled. He took off again in his slow, sleepwalk stride as Simone and Chim Chim stared after him.

"Well, if that isn't the strangest thing I've seen all week," Chim Chim said. She shook her head as she turned toward the pet door.

"Yeah, Jack must not be feeling well today," Simone agreed. "We'll catch up with him next time." She studied the package again. "This box is small enough. I'm going to push it through the pet door so it doesn't get stolen by some passerby. It could be pet *treats*, you know." She wiggled her eyebrows.

"It's probably only flea medicine, but suit yourself," Chim Chim said. She pushed back through the plastic flap.

Simone shrugged. She knew Audrey often ordered pet supplies online, as Dr. Edwards had gotten quite expensive since his veterinary practice first opened in Valencia Springs six years ago. She had overheard Audrey tell her sister that he'd probably raised his prices to pay for his "fancy new clinic" that was built last summer. "Glamour costs money," Audrey had said. "But he's the best vet in town, so I'll just have to cut costs where I can."

Simone leaned down and pressed her nose against the brown cardboard while walking slowly forward. When she reached the pet door, she rocked the box forward onto its corner and gave it a nudge. It fell through the pet door with a soft thud. She followed through the flap and stepped around the package, careful to leave it where it lay. Audrey was used to her young cats being clever—and helpful—but Simone didn't want to press her luck. It was best to let her owner think the postal lady had pushed it inside.

She rejoined Chim Chim on the patio table and finished her bath. She couldn't help but wonder what was wrong with Jack. They should probably check on their little neighbor in a day or so to make sure he was feeling better. She made a mental note of it as she curled up for a nap.

CHAPTER 3

Home Sweet Home?

A slight breeze blew through the screened walls of the Florida room, making the warm air quite pleasant. Wispy, white clouds laced the perfect blue of the fall sky as Chim Chim lounged on the patio table the next afternoon. She raised her head as the shrill ring of the telephone invaded her peaceful solitude. She knew Simone was inside and probably listening, so she decided not to concern herself. She rested her head on her forepaws and prepared for a snooze.

A few seconds later, Simone pushed through the pet door and padded over to the table.

Chim Chim opened an eye at her approach. "Anybody important?" She knew the call hadn't been for Crime Busters, as the caller hadn't used their secret ring pattern of two rings, hang up, and an immediate call back.

"I'd say so. It was Dr. Edwards's office."

"Really?" Chim Chim asked, pulling herself to a sitting position. The mere mention of her veterinarian's name made her feel anxious. "Nothing bad, was it?"

"No—in fact, I just overheard *good* news on the answering machine," Simone said, smiling.

"Yeah?" Chim Chim asked. Her tail twitched as she tried to be patient, but Simone was taking her time getting around to it. "Well?"

"Stacy, the vet tech, called to say that Zoe is ready to be picked up today."

"Zoe is coming home . . . *today?*" Chim Chim couldn't help the grin that spread across her face. "That *is* good news!" She frowned suddenly. "Do you think Audrey knows to pick her up?"

"I would think so," Simone said. "The message said they'd try her on her cell phone."

"Good." Chim Chim nodded excitedly. "Then we need to get ready!" Chim Chim felt a sudden sense of panic. She jumped down from the table and began to pace. "We should clean up our feeding area, and um . . . make sure Audrey has plenty of Zoe's favorite food. And I need to groom a little better—she said last year that my grooming habits weren't, uh . . . well, as good as hers. We don't have time to waste!" She shot up the step and through the inner pet door before Simone could utter a word of protest.

A couple of hours later, an exhausted Chim Chim joined Simone on the couch. All her homecoming chores were finally done, and everything was clean. Simone looked relaxed and refreshed as she watched a show on television. *Must be nice*, Chim Chim thought. *I always get stuck doing all the paw-work.*

She cocked her ears toward the kitchen as the bell-like ring of the telephone sounded. After four rings, Audrey's answering machine picked up. Chim Chim held her breath as an unfamiliar male voice started speaking.

"Yeah, Audrey? It's me—Neal. I thought you'd be home by now. I'll, um . . . try your cell phone. Bye." A click sounded as the caller hung up, followed by the loud *beep* of the answering machine.

Chim Chim turned to Simone with narrowed eyes. Her nose wrinkled in distaste.

"He's been calling more often lately," Simone said.

"Yeah, well, I don't like it one bit," Chim Chim said. "We don't need another human in our lives—things were just fine before he came along. Besides, he must not be too important to Audrey, or he would have known she was picking up Zoe, right?"

"Possibly." Simone shrugged and turned back to the television.

"What are you watching, anyway?" Chim Chim asked, turning her attention to the human on the program. He was speaking directly into the screen with a lively, animated expression. The cameras then panned to show the audience giving a large round of applause as the closing music started.

"Dr. Claws," Simone said. "He was showing the

audience how to create pet-friendly exercise areas inside their homes."

"Oh, yeah. Interesting," Chim Chim mumbled. Honestly, it didn't sound the least bit interesting to her, but she didn't want to hurt Simone's feelings. She curled up in a comfortable position with a good view of the TV screen. Her ears cocked as a commercial came on with a catchy jingle.

"Find your pet is too upset? We've got the best answer yet. Tran-quil-ta." ♪

Chim Chim stared as the screen filled with images of happy owners at a dog park. Their pooches blissfully wagged their tails and sprinted with other dogs across the perfect green grass. The commercial ended with an elderly woman sitting in her armchair by a crackling fire, her beloved cat curled peacefully on her lap.

"Are you *kidding* me?" Chim Chim exclaimed.

"You haven't seen that commercial before?" Simone asked.

"No, never."

"I've seen it a couple of times," Simone said. "It started playing last week."

"Well, I don't care if I *ever* see it again," Chim Chim declared. "Nobody's life is that perfect—with or without medication."

"No," Simone agreed, "it's not."

Suddenly Chim Chim remembered something. She leaped off the couch and dashed back into the kitchen. She stood on her hind legs and rummaged around the trash can with a forepaw until she found a familiar piece of folded paper. Digging her claws into it, she pulled it from the can and laid it on the floor. Then she grasped the paper gently in her jaws and carried it in to Simone, dropping it on the couch between them.

"What is it?" Simone asked, cocking her head.

"Read it," Chim Chim urged, unfolding it with a paw.

"Introductory special," Simone began. "New Tranquilta! Helpful for eliminating unwanted pet behaviors. Reduces hostility, fear, and anxiety in cats and dogs." Simone paused, arching an eyebrow. "Only $49.00 for initial month's supply. Money-back guarantee if not satisfied with the product."

"I thought that name sounded familiar!" Chim Chim said. "It makes me want to vomit."

"Where did you find this?" Simone asked.

"It must have come with the package that was delivered yesterday—which *was* flea drops, by the way." Chim Chim tilted her chin, gloating. "Audrey left it beside the box." She chuckled. "So I put it directly in the trash."

"Good. We don't need her getting any bad ideas."

They were interrupted by the loud clanging of the garage door opening. "They're home!" Chim exclaimed, bolting upright. She leaped off the couch, leaving Simone to turn off the television, and sprinted into the kitchen to wait.

Simone joined her by the food bowls, appearing to study her for a moment. The white cat raised a furry brow. "Am I wrong, or are you actually excited that Zoe is home?"

"Well, yeah . . . I guess I did miss the old bat," Chim Chim said casually. She wasn't about to admit how much! "There hasn't been anyone to snap at me during breakfast."

"Mm-hmm," Simone said with a knowing grin.

"Shh! Here they come."

They heard a jingle of keys, and then the door from the garage opened. Audrey emerged, struggling to juggle keys, purse, and cat carrier. She set the carrier down with a thud. "Sorry, Zoe."

"Hmph!" Zoe snorted, her tone regal.

Audrey leaned down and hit the latch on the carrier. The metal door swung open, and Zoe peered out before placing an elegant paw outside the crate. Zoe was a *torti*, or "tortoise-shell," known for her distinct black-and-gold coloring. The elderly cat tested her weight on the extended paw. She seemed unsteady at first; then she slowly emerged.

"Hi, Zoe," Chim Chim said, trying not to sound too eager. "Welcome home!"

"Junior," Zoe said with a solemn nod.

Chim Chim couldn't tell if Zoe was equally happy to see her.

"Welcome back, Zoe," Simone said with a smile.

"Thanks, Simone," Zoe said, stopping to stretch her front leg muscles. "Infernal plastic boxes."

"I know what you mean," Simone agreed. "They definitely weren't designed by a cat!"

"No, they weren't," Zoe said.

"Are you feeling better?" Chim Chim asked, not wanting to be left out.

"I'm tired, Junior. Really tired," Zoe said with a sigh. "I'm not throwing up anymore, but I have no energy at all."

Chim Chim gave what she thought was a look of deep sympathy.

"Well, you need to rest up," Simone said. "Later, we have some interesting news about Audrey to share with you. But for now, you need to get back to feeling like your old self."

"But she doesn't mean *old*," Chim Chim said. "Cause we'd never call you *old*."

Zoe raised an eyebrow.

"She knows what I meant, Chim Chim," Simone said, frowning.

Chim Chim dropped the subject. She was only trying to be helpful.

"Yes, ladies, I need to rest," Zoe said. "I promise I will visit more with you tomorrow."

"Of course," Simone said.

"Rest all you need," Chim Chim offered.

Zoe gave them a nod. Then she turned and padded slowly down the hall toward the bedroom.

CHAPTER 4
Bad Tidings

Simone sprinted across the flowery meadow. Butterflies rose as she passed them, startled by her pursuit of the tiny gray mouse. The sun shone warm upon her fur as she narrowed the gap between herself and her prey. She gathered her leg muscles for the pounce of victory, her heart pounding in anticipation— and was rudely snatched from her dream as an unearthly sound hit her ears. She lifted her head, ears cocked in the direction of the hallway outside Audrey's bedroom. She knew it wasn't part of her blissful sleep, but she wasn't quite sure *what* the sound was. Then she heard it again—kind of like the upchuck of a hairball, only louder, more violent.

She rose quickly and leaped from the bed, sprinting into the hall in search of the noise's source. As she turned the corner, she found Zoe huddled over a pool of vomit. The elderly cat's head hung low, her black-and-gold sides heaving as another spasm hit her.

Simone padded over to Zoe and waited for her to catch her breath. Then she placed a paw on Zoe's shoulder. "Are you all right?"

Zoe raised her head and turned to Simone. Her face was the picture of misery, with her golden eyes watering and spittle hanging from her furry chin. She took a ragged breath before speaking. "Yeah . . . I think . . . I hope so."

Behind them, Simone heard the soft thud of footsteps on the carpet. "Zoe? Are you—oh, no. Not again." Audrey gave a heavy sigh as she looked down at Zoe and the mess on the floor. She picked up the torti cat and held her close. "Baby, I just—I don't know what's wrong with you." Her breath caught in a gasp as tears flooded her eyes. She disappeared with Zoe down the hall.

Chim Chim soon appeared from the bedroom. "She's sick again, huh?" she said, more a statement than a question.

"I'm afraid so." Simone's heart felt heavy as she turned and followed Audrey into the kitchen. She heard the soft paw steps of Chim Chim behind her.

Audrey gave Zoe another hug and set her down gently on the floor. She picked up the telephone and quickly punched in a number—Simone assumed it was the number to the vet's office—and waited to record her message. She spoke in hushed tones, although Simone didn't know why, since everyone in their house was now out of bed. "This is Audrey Tanner. Zoe is throwing up again, and I—I don't know what to do." She choked back a sob on the last word, then gave her phone number and hit the "end" button on the phone.

Audrey looked down at Zoe, her eyes still brimming with tears. "The answering service will page Dr. Edwards. He should call us back in a few minutes." She reached to turn on the coffeemaker.

Simone glanced at the blue clock on the appliance. It read 5:32 a.m. Audrey was seldom out of bed before 6:00, but there would be no more sleep for any of them that morning.

Five minutes later, the shrill ring of the telephone made them all jump, even though they'd been expecting it. Audrey rushed to grab the phone from its cradle. "Yes, this is Audrey. She's stopped vomiting . . . for now. Yeah, I can have her there by 7:30. Thank you, Doctor," she said with a somber half-smile. "Okay, bye." She pressed the call-end button and placed the phone back onto its cradle. Pouring some coffee into a mug, she added sugar and took a deep gulp. Steam rose from the cup when she set it down.

"I guess I'd better clean up the mess and get a shower," Audrey said, looking down at them. "Hmm." She darted down the hall and reappeared with a bath towel from the laundry room. Then she scooped up Zoe and carried her to the living room. Simone followed, peeking around the corner, as Audrey laid Zoe gently on a towel she had spread across the couch cushions. Zoe curled up and tucked her tail under her chin.

Simone rejoined Chim Chim by the food bowls. Audrey hurried past them with cleaning supplies and a plastic grocery bag.

"I'm not chasing *anyone* around at this hour of the morning," Chim Chim declared, stretching.

Simone nodded. Chim Chim was definitely *not* a morning animal.

Audrey returned with the bagged mess and threw it in the kitchen trash can. Then she poured some kibbles into their bowls and left to get her shower.

"See?" Chim Chim asked. "Patience has its rewards."

Simone shrugged. She went through the motions of eating breakfast, although she had no desire for food. The dry cat food kibbles, normally quite tasty, seemed as bland as cardboard. She sighed, glancing over at Chim Chim. Her little buddy had cleaned her bowl entirely. Not much stood between Chim Chim and her stomach.

Audrey appeared a short while later. She was dressed for work and held an empty cat carrier in her right hand. Setting it down on the linoleum floor, she strode past them and returned with Zoe, using both hands to place the torti cat carefully into the plastic container. "I'll see you this evening, girls," she said with a grim smile.

Picking up the cat carrier with a groan, Audrey shifted her weight as she fumbled with the door leading out to the garage. She pulled the carrier in close to her body, but she still bumped it on the narrow doorframe as she stumbled through. "Sorry, Zoe!"

The door slammed shut behind her, echoing through the silent house.

Simone sat in front of the evening news as Audrey cooked dinner in the kitchen. Beside her on the couch, Chim Chim lay snoozing. Her little buddy seemed in low spirits since Zoe had returned to the veterinary hospital. She had slept a lot that afternoon and shown no interest in her catnip mouse.

They all were burdened with sadness that evening. Audrey trudged about the kitchen with a frown and her shoulders slumped—even a call from her new boyfriend had failed to improve her mood.

Simone frowned, too, as she turned back to the television. The weatherman from Tampa Channel 6 appeared on the screen, pointing to a map of the eastern United States and the islands below it. A tropical depression in the Caribbean Sea had been upgraded to a tropical storm, which meant it was gaining strength. It had crossed over the southern islands of the Bahamas earlier that morning and was headed on a direct course for Florida.

"Great," Simone muttered. "That's all we need to add to our worries." Tropical storms in late October were rare, but definitely not impossible. Simone hoped it wouldn't strengthen to a hurricane.

"What's great?" Chim Chim asked sleepily. Her eyes remained closed.

"A tropical storm is heading our way."

Chim Chim's eyes flew open. She sat up, just as Audrey appeared in the doorway.

"*Really?*" Audrey asked, listening to the weatherman. "And it's almost November? Ugh!" She stomped back into the kitchen with an exasperated sigh.

"Ditto that," Chim Chim said. "I hope Zoe doesn't have to wait out this storm at the vet's office. That would be scary for her."

"Yes it would," Simone agreed. She hoped so, too—for Zoe's sake. "The storm is forecasted to hit the eastern coast of Florida in three days, but these storms can change course several times before making landfall."

"That's not very comforting."

"No, but Audrey will keep the weather station on continually to monitor the storm's progress," Simone assured her. "That's what she's done in the past."

Chim Chim nodded, seeming satisfied with her response.

Simone hoped they wouldn't be affected too much. She remembered Audrey talking about the year 2004, when the eyes of three major hurricanes crisscrossed through the center of the state. She shuddered to think of it.

The news program ended, and a familiar jingle started. *"Find your pet is too upset? We've got the best—"*

Simone quickly changed the channel with a tap of her paw on the remote. "Ugh!" She glanced at Chim Chim, frowning. "I'm not sitting through *that* commercial again." Her eyes widened suddenly as she remembered that Audrey was in the next room. She turned, breath held, but Audrey was busy stirring a pot on the stove. The exhaust fan was running, so it probably masked any sounds from the living room. Simone exhaled slowly. She definitely didn't want Audrey to know she could operate a remote control.

Chim Chim giggled. "And you say *I'm* the careless one."

"Yeah, yeah," Simone muttered. She jumped down and padded into the kitchen to watch Audrey. The smell of burnt food explained the use of the exhaust fan. Her owner seemed distracted, but with good reason.

"Hello, baby," Audrey said, looking down at her. She gave Simone a grim smile and reached down to pet her head. "I miss her, too."

Simone tilted her head upward as Audrey rubbed under her chin. Although the attention felt good, she had entered the kitchen with a purpose. Sometimes it was a pet's job to ease her owner's sadness, to distract her human—or *humans*—from their pain.

Audrey's spirits seemed to lift a bit. She went back to her cooking without the frown, and her brow was no longer furrowed. Mission accomplished. Simone returned to the living room as the weatherman on the new channel showed the possible tracks of the approaching storm— and one of them went right through Valencia Springs!

CHAPTER 5

Cat's Eye of the Storm

Chim Chim watched from the kitchen as Audrey hauled in cases of water from her car. On the counter lay an assortment of hurricane supplies that her owner had already brought in the day before: D batteries for the flashlight, AA batteries for the weather radio, candles, and a candle lighter. The fridge was already stocked with extra milk and bags of ice, in case they lost electricity, and Audrey's bread box was stuffed full.

Tropical Storm Shelby had been upgraded to a hurricane that morning, according to the news channel. "That means the winds have strengthened, now that the storm is moving back out over open water," Simone had explained.

"Strengthened?" Chim Chim's eyes widened. "That's not good, is it?"

"No," Simone said. "But it's normal for tropical storms."

Mr. Faulkner had helped Audrey bring in her patio furniture that morning. They had stored it in the garage so it couldn't be tossed around by strong winds. Neal, her boyfriend, was coming over after lunch to help her board up the windows and sliding glass door with large sheets of plywood—which Audrey had already picked up from the hardware store. Chim Chim was looking forward to finally laying eyes on this mystery guy! Neal had promised to come the day before, but he'd called it off, making excuses about his job—or was it his stomach? She couldn't remember.

Audrey had been given the day off from work. Luckily for the cats, she was a worrier, and worriers *always* prepared for impending danger. Chim Chim had seen evidence of what happened for the humans who didn't. The Orlando news channel had shown footage of store after store with empty bread and water shelves, along with people fighting for the last pieces of plywood. *Geez!*

Simone joined her in the kitchen as their owner brought in the last case of bottled water. Audrey dropped it on top of the other cases she'd stacked in the corner. *Thud!*

Chim Chim found all of this mildly exciting. She'd never been through a hurricane before. "Have *you* ever been through one of these storms?"

Simone touched a paw to her chin. "Yeah . . . well, almost," she mused. "The summer when I was a kitten, I seem to remember a tropical storm was heading our way—but it ended up making landfall much farther north. Then when I was about three, we had to prepare for another tropical storm. I've never been through a direct hit, but still . . . the preparations are always the same. These storms have a mind of their own, so it's better to be prepared, just in case."

Chim Chim nodded. She and Simone followed Audrey into the living room to check for storm updates. Channel 6 out of Tampa was on, but her owner grabbed the remote control and changed it to the 24-hour weather channel. Audrey's favorite meteorologist—or weatherman—was broadcasting from Vero Beach. The fierce winds blasted him with sea spray as he stood several yards from the ocean's edge. The storm was still one hundred miles off the coast, but the waves were already beating furiously at the shoreline. The beach was eerily empty; no other humans were out, and no birds attempted to fly in the path of the storm. All living creatures had bunkered down to wait it out.

Chim Chim was glad they didn't live on the coast. Sure, it was pretty, but the need to evacuate—to leave one's home—every time a strong storm came through would get old pretty fast. Then, the process wouldn't be mildly exciting—it would be *terrifying*.

The meteorologist's words were interrupted by the sudden ring of the telephone. Audrey tossed the remote onto the couch beside Simone and darted into the kitchen. Chim Chim and Simone listened from the living room.

"Hi, Neal," Audrey said. "No, not yet . . . I was waiting for *you*. No, I can't board them up by myself." She sighed. "I understand. Yeah, I'm sure Mr. Faulkner will help me."

Chim Chim could hear irritation growing in Audrey's voice. She snuck a sideways glance at Simone.

"I wonder what his excuse is *this* time," Simone said, echoing her thoughts.

Chim Chim shook her head. She was sure it was something lame.

"No, I'm fine here," Audrey said. "I don't want to leave the girls by themselves. It's bad enough Zoe is all alone at the clinic." She paused. "Okay, I'll check in with you later." Another pause. "Miss you, too. Bye."

Chim Chim stuck out her tongue and made a loud gagging noise to show her disapproval.

Simone pressed a paw to her lips, widening her eyes at Chim Chim as Audrey reentered the room.

"Chim Chim? Are you okay?" Audrey asked, arching an eyebrow. "Looks like we're on our own, girls—at least we have good neighbors." She attempted a smile. "Guess I'd better call Mr. Faulkner again." She gave a heavy sigh and trudged back into the kitchen.

"That figures," Simone said.

"Yeah. I'm really beginning to dislike this Neal guy," Chim Chim said, frowning. She turned her attention back to the television. A short news spot discussed pet safety during tropical storms, making her heart feel heavy. "Do you think Zoe will be all right by herself?"

"I'm sure she'll be fine," Simone said. "She's a lot older than us. She's probably been through a bunch of these storms already." She gave Chim Chim a reassuring smile.

"Yeah, probably." Chim Chim didn't feel assured, but there was nothing she could do. Like the others, she was forced to wait it out. She lay down and rested her chin on her forepaws as the weather station cut to a commercial break.

Chim Chim was awakened by the sound of strong winds rattling the screened walls of the Florida room. Everything was shrouded in darkness, but her feline eyes adjusted quickly to the lack of light. The power had gone out close to midnight as Audrey finally fell asleep on the couch. Their owner had spent the evening glued to her favorite weather channel, watching the track of Hurricane Shelby. It had gone ashore north of Sebastian Inlet and weakened to a tropical storm, but the meteorologist said the sustained winds would still reach thirty-six miles per hour, with gusts even stronger. The eye of the storm had taken a northwestern track, so Valencia Springs was no longer in its direct crosshairs. But they would still be affected by the outer storm bands south of the eyewall.

Chim Chim rose from the couch and padded over to the sliding glass door. She tried to peek outside, but plywood completely covered the glass from top to bottom. She stepped toward the pet door and pressed on the opaque plastic flap, but it wouldn't budge. Audrey must have locked it to prevent them from going out during the storm. Simone would have scolded her, anyway, for placing herself in harm's way.

Chim Chim's breath caught as another wind gust rattled the Florida room. She hoped that the metal frame holding the screened panels would hold up against the gale. She would hate to lose her favorite napping spot.

She padded over to the front living room windows. Nosing behind the curtain, she rose on her hind legs and rested her forepaws on the window sill. She peered through a tiny gap at the bottom of the plywood that covered the windows. It was a small opening, but if she pressed her nose to the window, she could make out Pine Street. Their neighborhood was completely dark— no electricity also meant no streetlights. But it wasn't a problem for her feline vision.

Fierce wind gusts bowed trees and shook the stop sign at the corner. Her eyes grew wide as a piece of debris from a neighbor's yard flew into their mailbox.

Rain pelted the plywood in a rhythmic pattern, similar to the sound of hoofbeats in an old Western movie. Glancing down, she could make out puddles of water in the low areas of Audrey's yard. She wished she had a better viewpoint! After a few minutes, her eyes ached from squinting, and the low angle of her lookout made her neck stiff.

She rejoined Simone and Audrey on the sofa. Only the light of morning would reveal the extent of damage caused by the storm. She lay back down, wishing they made earplugs for cats. She cringed at every gust of wind, imagining it to be ripping off an important part of the house. *Was that a piece of the roof? Did our neighbor's awning just tear through the screened room?* Her heart raced, but try as she might, she couldn't calm down. She closed her eyes with a sigh. It was going to be a long night.

CHAPTER 6
Damage Control

Morning came, and sunlight began to peek through the remaining clouds of the storm. The winds were much lighter now, with only occasional gusts. And the rain, which fell in periodic bursts, was light.

By noon the clouds had given way to mostly blue skies, allowing the sun to reign again. Simone followed Audrey as she sloshed around their soggy yard, looking for signs of damage. The Florida room had survived the storm, with only a small tear in one of the screens. But the towering hibiscus bushes at the edge of Audrey's property were bent over, their blooms long gone. Audrey's other flowers—lively purple Mexican heather planted below the front windows—also showed wear from the strong winds.

The back yard was in worse shape. The canal at the southern edge of their property had overflowed its banks, and the low spot where the orange trees were planted held six inches of water. Simone knew that in a few days, the Florida sun—reaching eighty-plus degrees, even in

October—would dry up much of the standing water in the yard. The canal, which was fed by Lake Marion, would probably take longer to recede. But in a couple of weeks, things might be back to normal.

Simone followed her owner as she trudged back through the wet grass to the front sidewalk. Audrey opened the screen door, pausing to look down at Simone with a grim smile. "It could have been a lot worse, huh? At least the house is okay. I'll get Mr. Faulkner to help me uncover the windows in a bit."

Simone stepped through the open door. She studied her paws as Audrey kicked off her dirty shoes. *Yuck.* Her toe pads were coated with the dirt-sand mix common in Florida yards, and her white fur was stained a light brown. With a sigh, she bent down to clean her feet with her rough, pink tongue. When she was finished, she pushed through the inner pet door and joined Chim Chim by the food bowls.

Audrey appeared from the hallway and grabbed the telephone from its receiver. She hit a button and listened, then laid the phone back in its cradle. "No power—right." She disappeared back down the hall, returning with her cell phone. She entered a number, chewing on her lower lip as she waited. "Nobody's answering at the vet's office." Audrey touched her phone with a fingertip to end the call. "Their power must be out, too." She glanced down at a notepad lying beside the phone. "Hmm." She called another number.

"I think it's the vet tech's cell phone number," Simone told Chim Chim, whose brows had furrowed.

"Oh." Chim Chim nodded.

"Hello, Stacy? Yes, this is Audrey Tanner, Zoe's owner. I was checking to see how she did during the storm." She sighed. "Yes, I know the staff was sent home for their safety. Yes, of course—well, how's she doing now? Okay, thanks."

Audrey covered the lower half of the phone with her palm and looked down at Simone and Chim Chim. "She's going to check on Zoe. She'll be right back."

"She knows we can't answer her, right?" Chim Chim asked.

Simone shrugged as Audrey put the phone back to her ear.

"Yes, Stacy. She's doing well? Great! When does the doc think she can come home? Oh, that's wonderful! Thanks so much. Good-bye." Audrey ended the call and laid her cell phone on the counter.

"She's coming home Friday, girls!" Audrey picked up Simone and gave her a warm hug, causing a purr to rumble in her throat. She then rubbed between Simone's ears before placing her gently back on the floor.

"Oh, I see how it is," Chim Chim said. "You get the hug of joy—and what do *I* get? Ignored, that's what." She snorted her displeasure.

"Give her a break. She's been—we've *all* been—through a lot in the past twenty-four hours," Simone reminded her little chum.

Chim Chim's irritation seemed to melt quickly as Audrey leaned down to fill their food bowls. The sound of crunching kibble soon followed. Simone shook her head. *Typical*

Chim Chim, she thought. She bent her head to her own bowl with a smile.

Thursday morning, Simone and Chim Chim perched on the glass-topped patio table as Audrey got ready for work. The dawn sky changed from dark gray to a lighter gray, and eventually to the palest of blues. The sun peeked over the horizon, painting the few light clouds a bold tangerine tinged with bright pink. The birds announced the sunrise with their joyful song. Simone breathed deeply, enjoying the cool morning air.

"Zoe gets to come home tomorrow," Chim Chim said, smiling. "Good thing they finally got the power back on. It's too bad Audrey lost everything in the fridge, though."

"Yes, that's unfortunate," Simone agreed. "I'm thankful *our* food comes in bags and cans."

"Me, too." Chim Chim's expression grew serious. The corners of her mouth turned downward as her brows knitted together. "I sure hope Zoe doesn't get sick again."

Simone sighed. "Yes—let's hope that this time, she's home for good."

"But we still don't know what was wrong with her," Chim Chim pointed out.

"Well . . . if you ask me, it must have something to do with those pills that Dr. Edwards sent home with her."

"Pills?" Chim Chim asked, cocking her head. "What pills?"

"I noticed Audrey placing a medicine bottle on the counter when she brought Zoe in last time." Simone lowered her voice. "I don't know what they are, but when Audrey leaves for work today, I'm going to do some snooping."

"You wouldn't be Valencia Springs's top detective if you didn't!" Chim Chim declared.

"Come on." Simone jumped down from the patio table and pushed through the pet door into the kitchen. She waited patiently as Audrey rushed around, pulling containers of food from the fridge and tossing them into her navy-blue lunch bag. Finally ready, Audrey grabbed her purse and car keys, bade them goodbye, and stomped off toward the door.

Simone gave Chim Chim a knowing look, causing them both to chuckle. They knew full well that their owner was *not* a morning person. Simone listened as Audrey started her car and the garage door rose with a harsh clanking sound. She gave Chim Chim a nod, and her little pal darted off to keep watch from the living room windows.

"Okay, Audrey's gone!" Chim Chim yelled after a couple of seconds. She returned to the kitchen. "We're clear."

Simone padded over to the pet food bowls. She knew that the cabinet behind the bowls contained their pet supplies. She opened the right-side door and began rummaging through its contents: cans, bags, extra pet food bowls—but no medication. She looked through the stuff on the left-hand side. Still nothing—not even their flea medicine. She knew the pill bottle had to be there somewhere.

Simone took a couple of steps back and sprang onto the countertop. Leaning over the edge, she pawed open the wide drawer at the top. *Bingo!* The drawer was filled with flea repellent drops, old flea collars, old rabies tags, and a prescription bottle of pills.

Simone rolled the bottle over with her paw and read the label:

> *Zoe Tanner*
> *Tranquilta*
> *Take one tablet daily at mealtime to reduce anxiety.*
> *3 Refills*

Simone gasped. "She wouldn't!"

"Wouldn't what? *Who* wouldn't?" Chim Chim asked.

"Audrey! Our beloved owner is the reason Zoe's been sick—she's *drugging* Zoe!"

It was Chim Chim's turn to gasp.

Simone and Chim Chim sat on the patio table in silence. What could they do? What *should* they do? Simone was at a loss for words. She *never*, in her wildest dreams, believed Audrey was capable of such an act.

The minutes passed. Finally Simone broke the stillness. "I can't understand why Audrey is giving Zoe this drug in the first place. It's one thing to take medication if you need it, but it's quite another to take meds when you're perfectly healthy and don't require any. Zoe doesn't have anxiety . . . or temper problems. Yes, she can be a bit grouchy in the morning—but so can Audrey."

Chim Chim snorted. "You've got *that* right!"

"But all reasons aside, I know what we have to do *first*," Simone said, jumping down from the table.

"What?" Chim Chim asked. "What do we have to do first?"

Simone heard a soft thud as she pushed through the inner pet door. She knew her little buddy was following behind her. "I'm going to do some research on this Tranquilta," she said, pausing in the kitchen. "We need to know what we're dealing with."

"Oh—good idea."

Simone padded down the hall and into the spare bedroom that served as Audrey's office, with Chim Chim close behind. "Get the lights, will you?" she asked over her shoulder. She booted up the computer with her nose, then waited as it whirred to life. She frowned, peering across the still-dark office. The tiny green lights on the computer and monitor gave off the only glow. "Having trouble?"

"No," Chim Chim said breathlessly, leaping at the switch. "I've . . . I've . . . got it!"

Simone grinned, remembering Chim Chim wasn't as tall as she was. She turned back to the computer as the lock screen appeared. She punched in the password with the tips of her paw pads. *C-H-I-M (space) C-H-I-M.* Then she hit "enter" with a chuckle. No, Audrey wasn't the most clever human on the block. But she always made up for it—until now—with a huge heart for animals.

Simone placed her paw on the plastic mouse with a sigh (how she missed the real thing!) and clicked on the internet icon. She entered *Tranquilta* in the search engine. A multitude of website links popped up pertaining to the drug. She tried a medical website first.

"What does it say? What does it *say*?" Chim Chim asked impatiently.

"Hold on—I'm still reading."

Chim Chim pushed in beside her.

"It says the FDA—the Food and Drug Administration— just approved Tranquilta in February of this year," Simone said. "So it hasn't been out on the market long."

"That's not good," Chim Chim said. "Any side effects?"

"Several. Nausea, *vomiting* . . ." Simone paused, raising her eyebrows as she emphasized the last word. "Along with seizures and temporary paralysis."

"Paralysis?" Chim Chim gasped. "As in 'not being able to move'? It's a miracle Zoe only threw up—it could have been a lot worse!"

"Indeed, it could."

"Sounds to me like the FDA should have banned it, not approved it," Chim Chim said.

"I agree," Simone said. "I can't believe Audrey even *thought* about giving such a drug to one of us. She must not have done any research herself."

"No. This isn't like her at all." Chim Chim shook her head. She turned to Simone, her eyes narrowing. "I bet it's because of that *boyfriend* of hers—she acts like a totally different person since she met him!"

Simone sighed. "Yes, she does."

Simone hit the "back" arrow and selected a link for a news story from March of that year. The headline read, *"New veterinary drug causes pet death in South Florida."* She gasped.

"What?" Chim Chim asked, squinting at the screen. "Oh, my!" Chim Chim's head bobbed back and forth as she scanned the article.

Simone nodded, clicking on the next page. "Look—it says that animal-rights groups are trying to get Tranquilta pulled from the market. It seems the clinical trials weren't thorough enough, and there are rumors that the results were faked to get FDA approval." She finished reading and arrowed back to the search screen.

"What if that drug kills Zoe?" Chim Chim asked softly. "I'd never forgive myself for being mean to her when I was younger."

Simone gave her buddy a pat on the shoulder. "Zoe is going to be fine, Chim Chim. We'll make sure of it."

She clicked on a couple more medical websites and scanned the statistics. "These all say pretty much the same thing. That leads me to believe this Tranquilta is *not* as safe as it claims." She exited the search engine and powered down the computer with a couple clicks of the mouse.

"I agree," said Chim Chim. "But how do we make sure Zoe isn't given this drug again when she gets home?"

"I don't know, little buddy." Simone shook her head. "But we'd better think of something—and fast."

CHAPTER 7
Garbage Disposal

Chim Chim woke the next morning feeling exhausted and out of sorts. She plodded wearily down the hall and joined Simone in the kitchen. Her muscles ached as if she'd run a marathon the day before.

"You don't look so good," Simone observed.

"Rough night," Chim Chim said. "I kept dreaming that Zoe was in danger, and no matter what I did, I was powerless to save her." She let out a heavy breath.

"It's all going to be fine," Simone assured her. "Zoe is coming home today. Besides, I have a plan." She beamed, looking proud of herself.

"You do?" Chim Chim asked eagerly.

"I do," Simone said. "We're going to get our paws on those pills before Audrey can give her any more."

"Or give them to *us*," Chim Chim added. She moved aside as Audrey leaned down to fill their food bowls.

"That's right," Simone said with a firm nod of her head.

Chim Chim chewed and swallowed a mouthful of food.

"So . . . when are we doing that?"

"When Audrey leaves for work today." Simone lowered her voice. "We're going to steal the pill bottle from the supply cabinet, and we're going to dispose of it."

Chim Chim thought she had heard her buddy wrong. "Dispose of it? Where?"

"I . . . um—I'm still working out the details," Simone said.

Chim Chim gave her a raised-eyebrow look. She knew she should have stayed in bed!

Chim Chim and Simone waited on the patio table as the sun rose higher in the sky. Audrey had been gone since 7:30 a.m., but Simone wanted to wait until 9:00, so more of the humans in the neighborhood would be at work.

Chim Chim jumped down and padded over to the step. She poked her head through the inner pet door to get a look at the kitchen clock. Then she drew back and turned to Simone. "Eight-fifteen. Too early?"

"Yes, Chim Chim. We need to wait until nine to be safe."

"Oh, yeah. Right." Chim Chim trudged back to the patio table. She rejoined Simone and lay down, resting her chin on her forepaws. She gave a deep sigh and closed her eyes. The cheerful song of the morning birds soon lulled her into a much-needed sleep.

She awoke sometime later with a start and peered up at the position of the sun. She jumped down again and pushed back through the pet door. "Eight-forty-five!" she called through the flap. "Still too early?"

"*Yes*, Chim Chim."

Chim Chim hung her head in defeat as she shoved back through the pet door. She hated waiting! She exhaled loudly and collapsed on the single step, refusing to move.

Simone glanced up and apparently decided to ignore her. The older cat began grooming her thick, white fur instead—but Chim Chim didn't miss the slight upturn at the corners of Simone's mouth.

A few short minutes later, Simone stopped grooming and leaped off the table. She padded over to Chim Chim with a smile. "You ready?"

"*Ready?* I've been ready for over an hour!" Chim Chim sputtered. Sometimes she believed Simone liked to aggravate her for the pure fun of it. She narrowed her eyes as Simone patted her on the shoulder. The older cat chuckled, pushing through the inner pet door with a *swoosh! Bat, bat, bat!*

Chim Chim gave a snort as she shoved through the plastic flap. She padded over to the pet supply cabinet, where Simone waited.

"Help me with the bottle?" Simone asked.

"Yeah, sure," Chim Chim grumbled.

Simone leaped onto the counter of the cabinet and leaned over the edge. She pawed open the drawer, then looked down at Chim Chim. "Get ready to catch it when it falls."

"Right."

Simone dug around the drawer, found the right pill bottle, and rolled it toward the front with her forepaw. She attempted to push it to the top of the drawer, but it fell back down with a clatter. Simone wedged her paw in again, but this time stuck her face in as well.

Chim Chim assumed she was using her nose to help roll it over the edge—or at least that's what *she* would do.

When Simone got the bottle to the top of the drawer, she gave it one last push with her nose. "Bombs away!" she cried.

Chim Chim caught it briefly with her paw, but it bounced out of her grasp and hit the linoleum floor with a crack and a rattle. "Oops."

"It's okay—at least you softened its fall," Simone said. "These bottles are pretty tough." She jumped down from the counter and grasped the pill bottle in her jaws.

"What are you going to do with it now?" Chim Chim asked.

"Mm mm, hmm mm mm," Simone said, her mouth full. She motioned toward the hallway with a jerk of her head.

"Huh?" Sometimes Simone made no sense—literally. With a shake of her head, Chim Chim followed Simone down the hall to the bathroom. Padding through the doorway, she saw Simone about to spring onto the toilet.

"You're not going to flush that, are you?" Chim Chim asked, alarmed. "Won't it clog the toilet?"

Simone paused, dropping the pill bottle on the rug. "Yeah, you're right."

Chim Chim was surprised Simone hadn't thought of that first. Her housemate was two years older—and usually the wiser one. Of course, Chim Chim had come a long way in terms of experience in the past year.

Simone looked down at the bottle, then back at Chim Chim. "I can't even get the safety lid off. I wonder how we can dispose of these in a safe manner."

"In the garbage?"

"Maybe," Simone mused. "But we'd have to hide the bottle inside something. Then Audrey won't see it if she goes digging."

"Unless we throw it in the outside trash bin," Chim Chim suggested.

"Or in *someone else's* trash bin!" Simone said with a gleam in her eye. "Care to take a walk?"

"Yeah, sure." Chim Chim wondered what she had in mind. She followed Simone back down the hall and out the pet door to the patio.

Simone jerked her head toward the door.

Chim Chim nodded, pushing through the second plastic pet door. She glanced in both directions as Simone joined her. "Okay, no one's around. Now what?"

Simone laid the bottle in the grass. "I think the trash bin behind the sales office might be a safe place," she said. "I'd throw the bottle in the canal, but if it's not watertight, the pills could contaminate the lake water."

"It wouldn't hurt Calvin to mellow out some." Chim Chim chuckled as she thought of their grouchy former client.

Simone grinned. "I agree, but we don't know if Tranquilta is intended for reptiles. It may impair an alligator's ability to hunt."

"Yeah, I didn't think about that." *But still . . .*

Chim Chim trotted beside Simone down Pine Street. The sun felt warm on her back—but not too hot—and the sky was a vivid periwinkle blue. A gray mourning dove perched on a power line overhead. *Woo-HOO-hoo-hoo!*

Many of the residents had already cleared their yards of storm debris, which they'd left in piles at the curb. This section of Highland Oaks didn't contain many trees, so there wasn't much brush to pick up. As they neared the corner of Hickory and Pine, Chim Chim glimpsed a familiar figure. "Hey, there's Jack." She sped up her pace to close the distance between them. "Good morning!" she called out to their neighbor.

The Jack Russell terrier sat under a stop sign, still as a statue. He turned his head slowly in their direction at the sound of her voice. "Oh . . . hello, Chim Chim."

Simone stopped next to him, dropping the pill bottle gently onto the grass. She furrowed her brows at Chim Chim and gestured toward Jack with her eyes.

Chim Chim agreed. Jack was still acting strangely. He was normally bursting with energy and nearly springing from the pavement. Now he seemed like a deflated balloon—or a sluggish python that has consumed a large meal.

"Jack?" Simone asked. "Are you okay?"

"Sure, Simone," Jack answered. "I'm just stopping for a rest. My owner will be calling me in a bit."

"A rest?" Chim Chim asked. "Since when did *you* ever need a rest?"

Jack blinked at Chim Chim as if he didn't understand the question.

"Never mind," Chim Chim said. She turned to Simone with eyebrows raised. Something was seriously wrong here!

Simone shook her head. "Well . . . enjoy the sunshine, Jack."

Jack stared blankly into the distance. "Oh, okay."

Simone knelt and grasped the bottle in her jaws.

"Later, Jack," Chim Chim said. She stole one last look at their little neighbor, then darted after Simone. They needed to figure out what was wrong with Jack, but first things first—they had to dispose of Zoe's pills and get home before Audrey returned from work.

Chim Chim and Simone crossed Hickory Street and continued down Pine. They slowed as they approached the Highland Oaks sales office at the end of the block. Chim Chim noticed the driveway was empty. *Good.* That meant the sales agent was out. With a nod, Simone started across the lawn. Chim Chim followed, treading through the thick St. Augustine grass. They stopped at the green plastic trash bin behind the building.

Simone rested the bottle in the grass and turned to Chim Chim, frowning. "Without pushing the bin over on its side—which would create too much noise—I don't see a way to get the lid open."

"Me, either," Chim Chim agreed. "What about the trash bin behind the clubhouse? It's bigger."

"Good idea. Let's go check it out." Simone grasped the bottle again, and they treaded back through the grass.

Chim Chim led the way across Pine Street to a sidewalk on the other side, which took them past empty tennis courts and the neighborhood pool. The pool area had also been cleared of debris from the storm, and the water was treated and clear. A handful of residents stretched out in lounge chairs, soaking up the October sunshine. No one looked up as they scampered past.

They followed the sidewalk to the Highland Oaks clubhouse, then stepped off into the thick grass. They padded around to the back of the building, where a large metal trash dumpster sat on a concrete slab. Chim Chim knew the humans held a lot of birthday parties and events in the clubhouse, so they probably needed a bigger container for trash.

Simone laid the pill bottle gently on the concrete. "This bin has a split lid," she observed. "Perfect. That will allow me to sit on one part of the lid while I hold up the other. Then you can jump up and drop the bottle inside."

"Sure, boss." It sounded like a good plan to Chim Chim.

Simone bunched her rear leg muscles and sprang onto the right side of the green plastic dumpster lid. Using her nose, she nudged the left side up a few inches. Then she stuck her head underneath to push it up higher. "*Eww! Gross!*" Chim Chim could see Simone's nose wrinkle at the smell that seeped out. "Okay, Chim." Simone's chest cavity expanded as she took a deep breath and held it.

Chim Chim knelt down and grasped the bottle gently in her jaws. She leaped onto the dumpster beside Simone and pushed her head under the open half of the lid.

Simone was right—the smell was overwhelming! Her nose crinkled as she gagged, accidentally dropping the bottle without looking down. It hit the bottom of the nearly-empty metal dumpster with a loud *clang!* Chim Chim jerked her head back and turned, wide-eyed, to Simone.

Simone's eyes mirrored her own. "Oops—I guess they haven't thrown out much trash this week!" She pulled her head back and let the lid fall as gently as possible. Luckily, the building blocked them from view of the street.

Chim Chim jumped hastily to the concrete below. They scurried back around the building and down the sidewalk, not slowing until they reached the pool. Chim Chim kept her eyes fixed firmly ahead as they padded silently past. She didn't want to make eye contact with anyone or draw any attention. She glanced back as they reached the end of the block, but no one was watching them. *Whew!*

Chim Chim and Simone crossed the quiet street and passed the sales office. Jack was long gone, so his owner must have retrieved him—or so Chim Chim hoped. In Jack's confused state, she didn't think it wise for him to be wandering the neighborhood alone.

They trotted the last block back to their house. Chim Chim pushed headfirst through the pet door and waited for Simone on the patio table. She gave a long exhale of breath. "Boy, that was close! I'm glad no one saw us."

"Me, too," Simone agreed. "I guess it would've been better to wait until there was more trash in the dumpster—but we couldn't risk Audrey giving more pills to Zoe."

"Definitely not. But it all worked out."

"Yes, it did," Simone said. She glanced at the clock. "Audrey's leaving work early to pick up Zoe, so we have a couple of hours until they get home. I'm going to clean this rotten garbage smell off of me first. Then what do you want to do?"

"*Meerkats* comes on at 12:00," Chim Chim said, giving Simone her best wide-eyed-kitten look and batting her lashes.

"Oh, okay," Simone said, laughing. "But tomorrow is *my* turn to choose."

"Of course," Chim Chim agreed. She joined Simone in grooming the traces of garbage from her fur. Dignified detectives should never smell like trash.

Once finished, Chim Chim jumped down from the table. "Last one inside is a rotten fish!" She dashed up the step and through the pet door, leaving her roommate to chuckle behind her.

CHAPTER 8
Hearing Is Believing

Zoe padded into the kitchen the next morning as Simone and Chim Chim were eating breakfast. The elderly cat had been weak when she first returned home, but Simone noticed she now moved with her signature regal gait—an indication she must be feeling better today. "Good morning, Zoe," she greeted.

"Good morning, Simone," Zoe said. "Morning, Junior."

Chim Chim, who'd been devouring her food as if it were the last morsel on earth, swallowed with a loud gulp. "Good morning!"

"Did you rest well last night?" Simone asked.

"Very much so," Zoe answered. "I feel almost like my old self." She nibbled a couple of kibbles from her bowl. "So what was the news you wanted to share with me before I got sick again?"

"Finish your breakfast," Simone said. "There's no rush. We can talk out in the Florida room when you're done."

Zoe nodded.

Simone gave herself a quick cleanup while her room-mates finished eating. Then she led the way through the pet door and out to the patio. She leaped upon the marine-print sofa and beckoned Zoe to join her. Chim Chim chose the matching chair.

"We found out why you've been so ill the past few weeks," Simone began.

"And you'll never believe it!" Chim Chim added.

Simone gave a sigh of impatience. "Chim . . . let me finish."

"Yeah, of course," Chim Chim said, hanging her head.

"Have you seen any of the commercials for a new veterinary drug called *Tranquilta?*" Simone asked.

"Maybe . . . um . . . I don't know," Zoe said.

Chim Chim cleared her throat and began to sing. *"Find your pet is too upset? We've got the best answer yet. Tran . . . quil . . . ta."* ♪

"Oh, yes! That absurd commercial with the syrupy-sweet happy pets prancing around," Zoe said. "It made me want to lose my breakfast."

"Well, it appears that our beloved Audrey has been giving this Tranquilta to you," Simone said. She raised an eyebrow for emphasis. "It has a short—but shady—history, and vomiting is one of its many side effects."

"Giving it to *me?* Audrey?" Zoe's eyes widened in disbelief. "How *could* she? Has she truly lost all her marbles?"

"Possibly," Simone said. "Chim Chim and I agree that this is completely out of character for her."

"It might have something to do with the funny way she's been acting," Chim Chim suggested.

"Funny?" Zoe asked, cocking her head. "Funny how?"

"Audrey has been, well . . . quite distracted lately," Simone said. "She's been singing a lot, and—"

"Completely neglecting us!" Chim Chim exclaimed.

"Yes," Simone said. "We think it's because she started dating."

"*Dating?*" Zoe asked. "As in, 'going out with a male of her species?'"

"Apparently so," Simone said. "It's too early to tell if the relationship is serious, but it has definitely affected her behavior toward us."

"You can say *that* again!" Chim Chim agreed.

"Hmm. What do we know about this . . . boyfriend?" Zoe asked.

"Not much," Simone said. "He's only been to the house once, and Audrey shooed us off to the bedroom. So we haven't laid eyes on him."

"Simone heard Audrey tell her sister that he has a good job, though—and he's cute," Chim Chim said.

"That remains to be seen," Zoe said. "But I'm glad she's found a nice guy. Audrey's been very good to us—to *all* of us. She rescued you from being drowned as the runt of your litter, Chim Chim. And she rescued *me* from a death sentence at the animal shelter."

"But that doesn't excuse her for giving you unsafe drugs!" Chim Chim exclaimed.

"No, it doesn't, Junior," Zoe said with a frown.

"Well, you don't need to worry about Tranquilta—at least not for the moment," Simone said.

"Yeah, we got rid of it," Chim Chim said proudly.

"Got rid of it?" Zoe asked, her jaw dropping. "How?"

"We disposed of the bottle in the dumpster behind the clubhouse," Simone said. "Audrey will have to buy more from the vet if she wants to give any to *you* again. And we'll be on the lookout this time."

"That's right," Chim Chim said. She gave a firm nod.

"Well, thank goodness you ladies were watching out for me," Zoe said. "I'd hate to think what would have happened if she'd continued giving me that horrid medication."

"No, we won't think about that," Simone said. "The important thing is that you're back home, safe and sound."

Zoe nodded, appearing to be deep in thought. "So back to this mystery boyfriend of Audrey's. . ."

"Neal," Chim Chim offered.

"His name is Neal?" Zoe repeated. "Hmm." A sly smile grew on the elderly cat's face. "My friends, don't you think it's time to find out what kind of human has entered our lives?"

Simone was intrigued. "What do you suggest?"

Zoe rubbed her chin with a black-and-gold paw. "I'd like to get a good look at this guy, but that opportunity may not present itself for a while. At the very least, I think we should listen in on their phone conversations."

Simone grinned. "A girl after my own heart!"

"Audrey has two phones—one in the kitchen and one by her bed," Zoe said. "So no matter which one she's talking on, that leaves us one to listen in on."

"But they're both cordless, so we'd have to be careful," Chim Chim pointed out. "She could walk around while she's talking."

"Quite true, Junior," Zoe agreed. "But we'll have to be careful either way."

Ring! Ring! Simone was roused from her pleasant nap by the high-pitched ring of the telephone. She glanced over at her sleeping buddy. "Chim Chim! Wake up! It might be Neal."

Chim Chim opened an eye and gave a deep sigh.

"Come on!" Simone jumped down from the patio sofa and dashed through the inner pet door without even a glance behind her.

Zoe waited by the kitchen phone, which had stopped ringing—meaning that Audrey had answered it in her bedroom. With a nod to Simone, Zoe gently eased the phone off its receiver and pushed the green button with an elegant paw. By this time, Chim Chim had joined them. They huddled around the phone, straining to hear.

"Yes, Neal." Audrey's soft voice sounded through the ear piece. "I should be able to join you and your sister on a cruise. It's only for a couple of days, right?"

A male voice answered. "Yeah, it's a weekend cruise, so the ship returns on Sunday."

"Will it be safe?" Audrey asked. "Next Friday is November 3, which is technically still in hurricane season."

"Definitely—there's nothing showing on the radar. Tropical storms are rare this late in the year. Hurricane Shelby was a fluke."

"Yeah, well, my odds are pretty good when it comes to flukes." Audrey gave a dry laugh.

"We'll be fine—don't worry. Besides, you need some time away. I've booked two cabins—one for myself, and one for you and Joyce."

"Oh, you shouldn't have. But I guess you're right. I could use some rest and relaxation in the sun."

"Then it's settled," Neal said. "Are you going to board the cats while we're gone?"

"No, I don't want to put them through that," Audrey said. "Zoe's had enough stress lately without me adding to it. I can pick up an automatic feeder for them . . . or ask my neighbor, Mr. Faulkner, to feed them while I'm gone."

"Yeah, sure," Neal said. "So how's Zoe doing, now that she's home?"

"Zoe? She's doing fine now."

"Have you started her back on the Tranquilta?"

Chim Chim gasped. Simone and Zoe turned to her, eyebrows raised. Simone put a paw to her lips. Chim Chim nodded.

"No," Audrey answered. "I haven't given her any more pills. I can't seem to remember where I left them. . ." She trailed off. "But don't worry—I can pick up more if I need them. Why are you so worried about Zoe, anyway?"

"Oh, I—I just don't want you to be under any more stress right now. That turnover at your job has made you anxious enough. Plus, I love animals, and I want what's best for her."

Zoe snorted.

"Did you hear something?" Neal asked.

"Maybe? I'm not sure," Audrey said. "Anyway, I need to go. I'll talk to you tomorrow."

"Okay, Audrey. Talk to you tomorrow. Love you."

All three cats gasped.

"Love you, too. Bye."

"Bye."

Simone hurriedly pushed the red call-end button and nudged the phone back onto its receiver.

"*Love?*" Chim Chim squeaked. "She's in *love?*"

"Oh, boy," Simone said, shaking her head. "I think we're in serious trouble, girls. And this may be just the beginning. . ."

CHAPTER 9

Trick . . . or Treat?

ing! Dong! The bell-like chime sounded throughout the house. *Ding! Dong!* Chim Chim's ears perked at the sound.

"Sounds like trick-or-treating has started," Simone said. "Luckily, there wasn't much storm damage, or the mayor would have cancelled it."

Chim Chim nodded. She watched as Audrey grabbed a bowl of candy from the hall table and opened the front door. Their owner was greeted with a loud "Trick or treat!"

Chim Chim edged closer to the door for a better look. A small group of children stood clustered outside. A purple glittery princess moved forward, her treat bag held open. "Trick or treat!" she repeated. Behind her, a pirate and zombie waited eagerly.

Audrey chuckled as she dropped a couple of pieces of candy into the princess's bag. "Thank you!" the child called out as she closed her bag and dashed down the driveway. The pirate burst forward to take his turn. "Trick or treat!"

Chim Chim glanced past the group of kids in her driveway. All along Pine Street children skipped and shuffled along, clutching bags, buckets, and plastic pumpkins. They wore an array of costumes: green-winged fairies, masked superheroes, vampires, ponies, and all sorts of scary creatures. Their parents followed closely behind, waiting discreetly as doorbells were rung and candy was handed out.

Chim Chim sighed. She loved the excitement of it all, but Audrey seldom let her out on Halloween—due to the superstition of black cats associated with the holiday. She backed away from the door and joined Simone at the kitchen window.

"This is killing you, isn't it?" Simone asked, eyeing her.

"No . . . I feel *peachy*. Just peachy," Chim Chim replied. She hoped her voice dripped with sarcasm, because she sure *didn't* feel "peachy."

Simone gave her a sympathetic look. "Maybe there's something we can do."

Chim Chim stared at Simone. "What do you mean?"

"Well, as long as you're not out by yourself, you should be safe enough—especially with all these human parents about."

"Really?" Chim Chim couldn't help but grow excited. She felt as eager as a kitten with a ball of string.

"Really." Simone smiled. "Audrey will be busy with trick-or-treaters at the front door, so we can slip out the other side of the house—through the pet door. We'll need to wait until the next group of kids rings the doorbell. Then we can hightail it down Oak to Elm Street. She'll never even see us leave."

"Thank you, Simone! Oh, thank you!" Chim Chim threw her front paws around Simone and gave her a delighted hug. Then she dashed out the pet door to the Florida room with a *swoosh! Bat, bat, bat!*

She waited by the outer pet door, breath held, as Simone joined her. A few short minutes later—but what felt like an eternity—the muffled chime of the doorbell sounded. *Ding dong!*

"There's our cue," Simone said.

That was all Chim Chim needed to hear. She burst through the pet door and down the sidewalk, not even looking back to see if Simone was following. She headed east on Oak Street and ran straight into a group of trick-or-treaters.

"Kitty!" a preschooler yelled, pointing at them. Chim Chim paused, regained her bearings, and shot past the crowd toward the end of the street. She could hear Simone closing in behind her.

They slowed as they passed Jack's house. Chim Chim noticed that Jack's owner didn't have his outside light on—a welcome sign usually given to trick-or-treaters.

"Mr. Faulkner must not be giving out candy this year," Simone said. "He's been pretty grumpy lately."

"I've noticed," Chim Chim said. "Poor Jack seems to catch the brunt of it." She saw no sign of their little neighbor, so she sped up the pace.

They passed two more groups of kids as they drew

closer to the end of Oak Street. Chim Chim paused under the stop sign at the corner.

"So, where do you want to go first?" Simone asked. "I would suggest that we stay within Highland Oaks."

Chim Chim nodded. She took a deep breath of the cool night air, feeling completely energized. "Let's circle the neighborhood and look for dropped treats." She glanced up at the darkening sky.

"There will be a full moon tonight," Simone said. "The crazies will be out for sure."

"Yeah," Chim Chim agreed. "We'd better not stay out too late."

They turned right on Elm Street and trotted toward the back of Highland Oaks housing development. Chim Chim looked up as they passed Kyle Stanley, one of the residents. He was out walking his Shetland sheepdog—the official name for a miniature collie.

"Evening, Dollie," Simone greeted.

"Evening, ladies," Dollie said in her very feminine voice. "You be careful, Chim Chim—you know it's Halloween night."

"So everyone tells me," Chim Chim mumbled, rolling her eyes. She quickly gave in to a smile. "Good to see you, Dollie."

The sheltie pranced past as Chim Chim and Simone continued down Elm.

"Dollie looked good," Simone remarked.

"That she did," Chim Chim agreed. She was glad the sheltie had been reunited with her owner after being kidnapped by Divinity Labs last year.

They took to a grassy lawn as a car passed. It drove slowly to avoid the groups of trick-or-treaters on the street. Chim Chim loved the hustle and bustle of Halloween night. Seldom did Highland Oaks have so much activity—even on Christmas.

The street lights switched on as Chim Chim and Simone reached Sycamore Street at the back of the subdivision. The homes on the south side of the street bordered Lake Marion, and Chim Chim could see that the water level was still high from Hurricane Shelby. The grassy lawns—once perfectly manicured—were now covered in a thin layer of sand and silt deposited by the receding floodwaters. Cleanup in this part of the neighborhood would take more time.

Chim Chim's feline eyes adjusted to the growing darkness as they neared Vervain's house on the right. Vervain was a German shepherd friend who had been extremely helpful on their last case—in fact, he'd saved Chim Chim's life! He was typical of the breed so often used in police work: lean and muscular, with a raspy voice and alarmingly sharp teeth.

As they reached Vervain's place, the tan-and-black dog burst down the driveway toward them, causing Chim Chim's tail to bristle. "Hello, ladies!" His face was lit in a smile that showed all his pearly whites. "It's great to see you out tonight!" His tail wagged furiously, and he practically bounced in his enthusiasm.

Chim Chim furrowed her brows. Something was extremely odd about this! Vervain lunged forward—causing a sharp intake of Chim Chim's breath and a rise of her fur—and softly touched noses with her. She jerked back, not knowing how to respond but feeling a strange anger rise within her. "Back off, buddy!" she declared. "Haven't you heard about 'personal space'? You're definitely violating mine!"

Vervain backed away. His head hung low and his smile had faded. "I'm sorry, Chim Chim. But I'm so *happy* to see you."

Chim Chim gave a deep sigh. "It's fine, Vervain. It's fine. Just, uh . . . watch how close you get next time. You realize I'm a cat, right? Not a dog?"

"Yes. Of course, of course!" Vervain's smile returned, along with the bounce in his step. "You ladies be careful tonight. If you need me, I'm only a bark—er, I mean, a *meow* away!"

"We will. Thanks, Vervain." Chim Chim forced a smile as she padded off. She turned to give Simone an exaggerated look with her eyes wide.

"What was *that* all about?" Simone asked.

"I have no earthly idea," Chim Chim said. "I've never seen Vervain like that. He's a German shepherd, for goodness' sake! They're usually ferocious."

"They are," Simone agreed. "Except for Caleb—he's pretty laid-back."

"Yeah, except for him." Caleb was Simone's friend at the police department. Chim Chim heard he was very nice.

As they rounded the corner and turned onto Pine Street, Chim Chim was drawn by the sound of music. "Ooh. . . let's check it out!"

"Sure—it's your night," Simone said.

As they drew nearer to the 300 block, Chim Chim could see a great deal of activity going on. Crowds of humans clustered around. The music that reached her ears—an eerie sort of organ music, accented by howling ghosts and wailing cats—was both inviting and terrifying. "Mmm," she purred. She breathed deeply of the sights, smells, and sounds.

"Go ahead," Simone said with a chuckle.

Chim Chim dashed ahead, stopping at the edge of the property. The busy house belonged to Davina Spellman, a single lady in her mid-thirties who worked as an advertising executive. And boy, did she know how to throw a Halloween party!

Chim Chim watched as kids grabbed candy from twin bowls guarded by a black-clad witch and a moving skeletal hand. Blindfolded children beat a pumpkin piñata. Adults took their turns lying in a pretend coffin that, when closed, shook, creaked, and billowed fog. Their excited squeals lured the braver children to give it a try. Punch bowls filled with a dark liquid and floating "eyeballs" lured thirsty passers-by. A snack table beckoned with popcorn balls, cheese stick "fingers," crispy rice cereal headstones, and candied apples.

Chim Chim salivated as she got a good whiff of the food. She looked around, trying to find Sabrina, Davina's Yorkie dog. Sabrina would help her get her paws on some of those cheese sticks! As her gaze traveled over the children and their parents, her eyes locked onto a familiar figure. The tall, athletic build and short, chestnut brown hair were unmistakable—even without the white lab coat. *Dr. Edwards!* What was *he* doing here?

She turned to Simone, who had caught up beside her. "What is Dr. Frankenstein doing in Highland Oaks?" She jerked her head toward their veterinarian. It was no secret that she didn't care for the guy.

"Hmm," Simone said. "I don't know." She shrugged. "He doesn't live here . . . and I don't think he has any kids."

"So no trick-or-treating."

"Right. We could follow him and see what he's up to," Simone suggested.

"My thoughts exactly." Chim Chim couldn't explain it, but her instincts told her not to trust the man. With a nod at Simone, she slinked past the legs of several adults, then past the group of kids clustered around the candy bowls. She took refuge under a table with bowls of creepy party favors and waited for her housemate.

A whoosh of air and the faintly nauseating odor of dog breath signaled the appearance of Sabrina beside her. The little Yorkie was no bigger than Chim Chim herself. Her fur was a light tan color, and she had fluffy tufts around her ears, tail, and feet. Her groomer had added tiny pink bows at each ear.

Sabrina gave a welcoming yip. "Hello, Chim Chim!" she said eagerly. Her tail wagged with excitement. "What are you doing out tonight? I'm surprised to see you here."

Chim Chim smiled as Simone appeared on her other side. "Well, you know I'm a black cat—and black cats *love* Halloween."

"Oh, yeah," Sabrina said in her squeaky, high-pitched voice. "I forget that sometimes." Her head bowed briefly as she chewed at something on her foot. "Hi, Simone."

"Hello, Sabrina," Simone said warmly.

Sabrina smiled, flashing a mouthful of tiny, sharp teeth. If she weren't so small, Sabrina would be fearsome.

"So . . . what are you staring at, Chim Chim?"

"Dr. Edwards, our veterinarian. I don't know what he's doing here, but he's got to be up to no good."

"Oh, yeah. I've only seen him here a couple of times," Sabrina said. "I think they're friends or something."

"Seems he has more friends than we gave him credit for," Chim Chim mumbled. "He's leaving the punch bowl— follow him!"

Chim Chim darted after their veterinarian, trying to keep up as she dodged clusters of kids and parents. Simone and Sabrina followed close behind. Dr. Edwards stopped at the candy table to speak with the costumed witch. *Ah . . .* Upon closer inspection, Chim Chim realized that the witch was actually Davina, Sabrina's owner. Dr. Edwards leaned closely and spoke to Davina, then motioned to the side with a jerk of his head. He walked over by the front door of the house, and Davina followed.

Chim Chim edged closer, but she was unable to hear their conversation. Davina laughed—a high, bell-like sound—and shook her long, blond hair. She put a hand on Dr. Edwards's arm and smiled, showing all her teeth. *Just like Audrey*, Chim Chim thought. She gasped, turning to her comrades. "Oh—they're dating! *Ugh!*" She stuck out her tongue in disgust.

"Wow. I didn't see *that* coming," Sabrina said, her eyes wide.

They continued to watch as Dr. Edwards pulled something from his pants pocket. He spoke briefly into Davina's ear and placed the item in the palm of her hand, closing her fingers around it. Then he kissed her on the cheek and strode off.

"Well, *that* was strange," Simone said. "I wonder what he gave her."

"Maybe it was money," Sabrina said. "Or free dog treats—like the kind they give out at the vet's office." She gave an excited "*Yip!*"

"Yeah, maybe," Chim Chim muttered. She doubted it was anything good, but she didn't want to ruin Sabrina's high hopes.

They trailed Dr. Edwards to the edge of Sabrina's yard. Chim Chim's gaze followed him as he crossed the street and climbed into his red sports car. He revved the engine to life, then sped off down Pine Street toward the Highland Oaks gate. His brake lights glowed in the distance as he came too close to a group of trick-or-treaters.

I hope they throw his butt in jail! Chim Chim thought, shaking her head. "Come on," she said, adopting a fake smile to hide her misgivings. "Let's get back to the party."

She led her companions back into the crowd.

CHAPTER 10
Maiden Voyage

A udrey took off from work early on Friday and pulled into the garage shortly before noon. Simone had overheard Audrey telling her sister on the phone that she and Neal were going to pick up *his* sister in Orlando. Then they would drive to Port Canaveral to board the ship for their cruise. Audrey—who was running late, as usual—now dashed around her room, throwing articles of clothing into her navy-blue, polka dot suitcase.

Simone watched from the hallway. Giving a sigh and a shake of her head, she padded through the kitchen to join her housemates in the living room. Zoe napped on the couch, her whiskers twitching, and Chim Chim stared at the television with a look of boredom.

"Well, girls . . . in half an hour we'll get to see this Neal character," Simone said.

"Neal, schmeal," Chim Chim said with a snort. "I don't like him already if he's pushing Audrey to give us bad drugs."

Zoe opened an eye. "I couldn't agree more, Junior."

Simone latched onto the remote with a paw, giving Chim Chim a wink. "Audrey's too busy to notice right now." She tapped the channel button until she found her favorite travel show. "Ooh. . . they're exploring Egypt. Did you know cats were revered there in ancient times? The killing of a cat was met with harsh punishment."

"Yeah, and I bet they didn't give their cats Tranquilta, either," Chim Chim said. She gave a firm nod of her head.

"Definitely not," Simone agreed. She lapsed into silence, listening intently to the program.

Twenty minutes later, they heard the low drone of an engine as Neal's vehicle pulled into the driveway. The shuffle of footsteps followed; then the doorbell rang.

Simone listened as Audrey's suitcase hit the floor with a thump. This was followed by the hum of rolling wheels—and a few more thumps—as their owner dragged the case down the hallway toward the door. Simone turned to her housemates. "Now's our chance."

She jumped down from the couch and scampered over to the kitchen island, which had the best view of the front door. She stayed out of sight, fearing Audrey might banish them to the bedroom again.

Chim Chim darted behind Simone, bumping into her.

"Chim!" Simone hissed. "Be careful."

"Sorry!"

Simone inched backward a couple of steps. She nodded at Zoe, who remained at the living room corner. They all waited, breath held, as Audrey grasped the doorknob and turned. The door opened inward to allow full view of her guest.

"Oh," Simone said, furrowing her brows. She'd expected this Neal-guy to look sinister, with big, bushy eyebrows and maybe a dark moustache. He had neither. In fact, his hairline was starting to recede and his remaining hair was already quite thin. His eyes were beady and too close together—like a rat's. Other than that, he looked very mild-mannered . . . and possibly nice. He wasn't overweight, but neither was he slim. He was average, all in all.

"Hello," Audrey trilled.

"Hello, Audrey," Neal said. He gave Audrey a quick kiss on the cheek. "Are you all packed?"

"Um, pretty much," Audrey said, glancing at her suitcase.

"Great. I'll carry it out for you," Neal said. He paused, pulling a prescription pill bottle from his pocket. "I stopped and picked these up at the vet for you." He placed the bottle in Audrey's hand. "These should hold Zoe over until we get back. Just leave a note for Mr. Faulkner to give her a pill with her breakfast each morning."

Simone and Chim Chim gasped.

Neal grabbed Audrey's suitcase by the handle and pulled it toward the door. He gave a slight groan as he jerked it over the threshold.

Audrey stared after him. "Oh, okay. Thanks." She frowned as she read the label on the bottle.

Simone listened to the clacking-hum of plastic wheels as Neal pulled the suitcase down the sidewalk to the driveway. When the humming stopped, she heard another groan, followed by the slam of the vehicle's rear hatch.

Audrey dropped the pill bottle into a small basket on the pet supply cabinet. She grabbed her purse and keys and gave one last look around. Then she followed Neal out the door, pulling it closed behind her. The deadbolt clicked as she locked it from the outside.

"So, what did you think?" Zoe asked, emerging from her hiding spot. She joined Simone and Chim Chim in the kitchen.

"It's hard to say," Simone replied. "He looked pretty normal to me." She shrugged.

"The eyes," Chim Chim declared. "Never trust a human with beady eyes."

Simone arched an eyebrow. "I thought you said all humans look alike, Chim Chim."

"Yeah, well . . . *this* one looks dishonest."

"Junior's right," Zoe said. "There was something I didn't like about him—something I can't quite pinpoint . . ." She trailed off.

"Well, beady eyes or not, we now know for certain he's behind the push to give Zoe drugs she doesn't need," Simone said. "And I'm sure he won't stop with just one of us."

"Can you believe he said on the phone that he *loves* animals?" Chim Chim asked. "What a big fake!"

"I agree, little buddy," Simone said. "We need to study this new enemy so we know what we're up against."

Chim Chim and Zoe nodded.

They listened in silence as Neal started his vehicle. The

drone of the engine grew louder as Neal backed out onto Pine Street. Then it faded as he and Audrey drove away.

"She forgot to write the note for Mr. Faulkner," Chim Chim realized.

"Oh, you're right," Simone said. "Good—that will buy us some time. The cruise ship doesn't return to port until Sunday evening, and they'll have a two-hour drive back. That gives us a couple of days to come up with a plan to get rid of Neal."

"And dispose of that new bottle of pills," Chim Chim added.

"That, my friends, will be *first* on my list," Simone said with a firm nod.

Simone woke later than usual Saturday morning. Soft sunlight filtered through the blinds in Audrey's bedroom and the muffled sound of birdsong reached her ears. She realized something was missing: no buzz of Audrey's soft snoring, no chaotic banging and thumping in the kitchen. The silence of the household was welcoming to her ears—and more favorable for sleep. It was definitely a change in their routine.

She stretched luxuriously, enjoying each flex of her muscles. Beside her, Chim Chim twitched slightly in her sleep. Simone decided to let her rest. She jumped down from the bed and padded quietly to the kitchen.

She glanced at the blue light on the coffee maker clock. *9:00 a.m.* Mr. Faulkner probably wouldn't come to feed them for another hour, so she pushed through the pet door out to the Florida room. Zoe had already risen and was giving herself a good grooming on the patio sofa. Simone padded over to join her.

"Morning, Zoe," she said, leaping onto the sofa printed with fish and tiny anchors.

"Good morning, Simone." Zoe paused from her cleanup. "Junior still sleeping?"

"Yeah, you know Chim Chim—*not* a morning animal at all." Simone chuckled.

"No, she sure isn't." Zoe smiled as she stretched her forepaws out before her. "The older I get, the less of a morning cat *I* am."

Simone smiled in return. She gazed down Oak Street toward Jack's house. She wondered if Jack would come with his owner to feed them. His behavior the past couple of weeks had been quite strange. She hoped he wasn't ill. She'd grown fond of their little neighbor and would hate for something bad to happen to him.

She stretched out on her stomach and listened to the morning songbirds. Even though she rarely hunted anymore, their chatter still stirred her senses. A car passed by on the street, briefly drowning out their song. Then it was quiet again. She rested her head on her paws to doze a while as she waited for breakfast.

Twenty minutes later, Simone heard a *yip* and the faint sound of a screen door slamming in the distance. She rose to a sitting position and glanced down at Zoe. Her elderly housemate was asleep, her paws twitching as she sighed.

Simone jumped down and padded over to the screen door to watch. The shuffle of feet, along with the clicking of toenails on asphalt, gradually grew louder. Soon Mr. Faulkner appeared with Jack on a leash. He turned up their sidewalk and approached the screen door, keys jingling in his hand. Simone backed up as he gave the door handle a tug. With a grunt, he tugged on it again, but it didn't budge—Audrey must have forgotten to leave it unlocked.

Mr. Faulkner muttered softly under his breath as he trudged back down the sidewalk to the street. He rounded the corner of the house, with Jack trailing behind him. The little terrier glanced back before they disappeared from sight.

Simone trotted over and pushed through the inner pet door to the kitchen. She waited by the center island as keys jiggled in the front door lock. The deadbolt turned and the door opened, allowing Mr. Faulkner and Jack entrance into the house.

Mr. Faulkner bent down and unhooked Jack's leash. "Now, don't wander off," he lectured—quite needlessly, as Jack stayed frozen in place, his eyes large and vacant.

"Good morning, Jack," Simone greeted.

Mr. Faulkner shuffled over to the pet supply cabinet. He rummaged around, looking for the container of cat food.

"Uh . . . hi, Simone," Jack said, turning slowly to face her. His eyes focused on her briefly, then returned to their vacant stare.

Simone furrowed her brows. Something was wrong. Very wrong. "Are you feeling okay, Jack?"

"Yeah, sure," Jack said. "I feel fine."

"Well, you don't *look* fine. Has Mr. Faulkner started you on a new diet? You're not acting like your normal self."

"New diet?" Jack repeated. "I don't think so. I'm getting my, um . . . my regular kibble at mealtimes. I think I'm getting a vitamin now, too—or maybe that was a treat. I'm having a hard time remembering."

"Well, maybe that's why he's giving you a vitamin," Simone suggested. "You might be deficient in something."

"Deficient?" Jack asked, cocking his head.

"Yes. That simply means you're low in some vitamin or mineral your body needs to function well. Your vet might have noticed it during your exam and prescribed something."

"Oh," Jack said, nodding slowly. "Yeah, that's probably it."

Simone looked up as her youngest housemate appeared in the doorway.

"Morning, Jack," Chim Chim greeted, giving a deep yawn and a stretch.

"Good morning, um . . . um . . ."

"Chim Chim, Jack—that's *Chim Chim*," Simone said, shaking her head. She laughed. "You *are* having a hard time remembering!"

Mr. Faulkner bent down with a groan and filled the three cat food bowls. Then he put the the plastic container of food back into the cabinet and rehooked Jack's leash. He started for the door but paused, looking back at them. "Enjoy your breakfast," he grumbled.

"Bye, Jack," Simone called after their friend. "I hope the vitamins help!" The door slammed in response.

"That sure was weird," Chim Chim said as the deadbolt clicked to its locked position. She padded over to their bowls.

"Indeed."

Zoe joined them in the kitchen.

"Well, what are we waiting for?" Chim Chim asked. "Let's eat!" She dove in immediately, not even pausing for breath.

CHAPTER 11
Pickpocket

The morning sun filtered through the screens of the Florida room as Simone cleared her throat. "I apologize for calling this meeting on a Sunday morning, ladies. But Audrey returns tonight, and we need to come up with a plan."

Chim Chim grunted. Simone had awakened her from a sound sleep and a pleasant dream with an enormous mound of fresh fish. Sundays were usually her day to sleep in, as Audrey was off from work and didn't have to set an alarm. Chim Chim felt cheated.

"I was already awake, so it's no bother," Zoe said. "But you're right—we need to figure out how to get rid of Audrey's new boyfriend. Were you and Chim Chim able to dispose of the new bottle of pills?"

"Yes," Simone said. "We had to dump them in the neighbor's trash this time, though. There was a birthday party at the clubhouse yesterday, with too many humans about."

"Well, at least they're gone," Zoe said.

Chim Chim gave an exaggerated yawn.

"Do you need some coffee, Chim Chim?" Simone asked, peering down her nose.

"Maybe." Maybe she *should* take up that gross human habit that Audrey loved so much!

Simone sighed. "Can we start now?"

With all eyes upon her, Chim Chim nodded.

"I've given this a lot of thought," Simone began, "and I've decided that the only way we're going to get rid of Neal—before we're *all* drugged—is for Audrey to realize what a horrible human he is. But she has to come to that conclusion on her own. All the people in the world can tell her this, but until she sees the evidence herself, she's going to be too starry-eyed to believe it. So . . . what we *can* do is dig up plenty of dirt on the guy. Then we leave our proof out for her to find."

"Good idea," Zoe said.

"How do you suggest we find this 'dirt'?" Chim Chim asked.

"I haven't figured that part out yet." Simone rubbed her chin. "Hmm. I heard Audrey say he lives outside the Valencia Springs city limits—close to the interstate. That's too far away for us to search his house, and we don't have any friends who could follow him from the air."

"We're not small enough to sneak into his car—like a mouse—and ride around with him, either," Chim Chim said.

"No," Zoe agreed. "Then we'll just have to spy on him while he's here."

"Or when he calls here," Simone said. "Sadly, we don't have the capability to place a wiretap on Audrey's home phone to record their conversations."

"And searching her cell phone wouldn't help," Zoe added. "I'm sure he only tells her—or texts her—what he wants her to hear."

"Definitely," Simone agreed. "I thought about e-mail . . . but when I checked her computer, I found that they rarely e-mail each other. Humans prefer to send text messages these days."

They thought for a moment in silence.

"What if we search *Neal's* phone?" Chim Chim suggested. "I bet there's a ton of stuff on his phone that he wouldn't want Audrey knowing about."

Simone's face brightened. "Excellent idea, Chim Chim."

"Brilliant, Junior," Zoe added.

Chim Chim puffed up a bit, enjoying the praise. "We'll have to swipe it while he's here, though," she pointed out.

"You're right," Simone said. "Well, Neal will be bringing Audrey home tonight after they drop off his sister. It may be our last chance for a while."

"Tonight it is, then," Zoe declared with a firm nod of her head.

Simone appeared thoughtful. "We'll need a distraction. Human males tend to carry their cell phones in their back pockets. So we need to find a way to get Neal's phone out of his."

"Ahem." Chim Chim cleared her throat, sitting taller. "Leave that to me."

＊＊＊＊＊＊

Chim Chim watched out the front window as the daylight started to dwindle. Audrey and Neal were due back any time now. She poked her head out from behind the curtains and glanced at Simone and Zoe on the living room couch.

"Any time," Simone said, echoing her thoughts. "Their ship should've made port two hours ago—and Neal's sister's house is on the way here."

Chim Chim nodded, turning back to the street. Within minutes, a white SUV appeared farther down Pine Street. She squinted, then relaxed her eyes as the vehicle drew closer. It passed Oak Street and slowed to turn into their driveway. "They're here!" she cried, ducking down and slinking out from under the curtain. "Showtime."

Chim Chim darted into the kitchen and waited behind the kitchen island for Simone and Zoe to join her. She could hear the sound of automobile doors opening and muffled human voices, immediately followed by the click-clack of sandals coming down the sidewalk.

"What do you have in mind?" Simone asked over Chim Chim's shoulder.

"You'll see," Chim Chim said. She gave Simone and Zoe a sly grin. "Be ready to grab the phone when it falls."

Keys jingled in the lock, and the front door burst open. Audrey dashed in, throwing both purse and keys onto the counter. She looked down at Simone and Zoe, who had wandered over to the food bowls. "Girls! Did you miss me?" She picked up each cat in turn and squeezed them tightly to her chest.

"*Oomph!*" Zoe appeared to lose her breath.

"Oh, sorry, Zoe!" Audrey exclaimed. "I should have been gentler—but I *missed* you all." She reached down and stroked the black-and-gold head. Zoe responded with a deep, gravelly purr.

Audrey looked around, her brows furrowing. "Where's Chim Chim?"

Chim Chim remained hidden, although the thought of a head rub was tempting. She heard the slam of the SUV's rear hatch, followed by the hum of suitcase wheels rolling up the sidewalk. She peeked around the kitchen island as Neal stepped through the doorway and paused inside. She frowned at the familiar beady eyes.

Audrey turned to her boyfriend. "Take it down the hall to my bedroom, if you don't mind, and throw it on the bed." She smiled sweetly. "Please."

"Sure thing." Neal tightened his hold on the handle of the suitcase and started down the hall. Suddenly Chim Chim zoomed out of the kitchen, darting between the man's legs again and again, before zooming off toward the safety of the bedroom.

Neal stumbled, cursing, and went down with a loud *thud!* He crashed onto the suitcase in a tangled heap.

Chim Chim watched from under Audrey's bed as a white blur flew toward the scene of chaos and snatched Neal's phone from the carpet where it had fallen. Grasping it in her jaws, Simone bolted down the hall and joined Chim Chim under the bed, just as Audrey appeared from the kitchen.

"Neal! Are you okay?" Audrey asked in horror.

Neal uttered a stream of swear words that made Chim Chim's mouth drop open.

Audrey's wide eyes revealed her shock at the change in Neal. But her expression quickly changed to a concerned frown. "I'm so sorry, Neal! I don't know what's gotten into them."

"Yeah, well . . . maybe you need to get better control of your animals," Neal grumbled as he rose to his feet and righted the suitcase. He dusted himself off, continuing to mumble under his breath. Grabbing the suitcase's handle, he pulled it the rest of the way toward the bedroom.

Chim Chim and Simone wriggled deeper under the bed so the beady-eyed human wouldn't see them.

Neal groaned as he lifted the suitcase off the floor. He threw it onto the bed with enough force to rattle the bedrails underneath, causing Chim Chim to jump. "I'll buy enough Tranquilta for *all* of them," he muttered under his breath. He turned and stomped back down the hallway.

Chim Chim and Simone both gasped.

CHAPTER 12
Digging in the Dirt

Simone and her housemates waited until Audrey was safely at work Monday morning. Simone had suggested they wait an extra half-hour after Audrey's departure, in case she forgot something and had to return. After what seemed like an appropriate amount of time, Simone jumped down from the patio table and dashed through the inner pet door to the kitchen.

She heard Chim Chim cry out behind her as she raced down the hall to Audrey's bedroom. "Slow down!"

They had stashed the phone deep under Audrey's bed between a Christmas wrapping paper tub and a sweater bag—neither of which would be touched anytime soon. Simone crouched down and crawled underneath. Sure enough, the phone lay where they'd left it. Grasping it carefully in her jaws, she wriggled out from under the bed.

Chim Chim waited for her in the kitchen, looking annoyed.

Simone trotted past her into the living room. She laid Neal's phone onto the carpet and held it down with one paw—so it wouldn't slide away—while pressing firmly on the side button with her other. She kept it pressed for three seconds until the phone powered up. A lock screen soon appeared, requesting a four-digit security PIN. Simone frowned. Audrey never locked *her* cell phone.

"Try his birth date," Chim Chim suggested, appearing over her shoulder.

"I don't *know* his birth date."

"Then try Audrey's birthday."

Simone entered *0-9-0-4* on the touch screen, then tapped "OK."

Incorrect PIN entered, the screen read. "That's not it."

"What about their dating anniversary?" Zoe asked. "Humans tend to think that's significant."

"Hmm." Simone rubbed her chin with a forepaw. "Chim Chim, go into Audrey's office and flip through the cat desk calendar her sister gave her. See if you can find anything she's written about Neal."

"I'm on it!" Chim Chim dashed out of the room. She returned a couple of minutes later with a small piece of paper clamped in her jaws. She dropped it on the carpet and grinned triumphantly. "This is the page from August 21. Audrey's written a note on it: *Double-date with Katherine.* She added Neal's name in parentheses out to the side."

Simone studied the paper. "Yeah, I think her friend Katherine introduced them. Good job, Chim Chim." She entered *0-8-2-1* on the touch screen. This time she was rewarded with Neal's home screen, which displayed a picture of Neal and Audrey on the beach. Audrey looked happy—she was smiling and showing all her teeth again. "Bingo!"

Chim Chim gagged as she stared at the photo.

"I couldn't agree more, Junior," Zoe said.

Neal's phone showed several missed calls. Simone had been careful to turn it off yesterday before he realized it was missing—and tried calling it. Luckily, he must not have had a phone locator app installed. "Let's see what this guy is up to." She narrowed her eyes at her housemates.

"No good, I'm sure," Chim Chim said.

Simone pressed her paw to the photo gallery icon on Neal's phone. She scrolled down, looking for pictures of Neal doing anything suspicious or illegal. The first dozen photos all seemed to be from his and Audrey's cruise. There were shots of them on the ship, shots of them on a quiet beach, and shots of Audrey with Neal's sister lounging by the shipboard pool. They must not have gone anywhere exciting—like the Bahamas. Neal was probably too cheap to pay for something like that.

She continued scrolling through his photos, losing interest, as the remainder of them seemed related to his work. Insurance wasn't very exciting. She sighed, about to press the "home" button, when something caught her eye. Squinting, she clicked on the tiny thumbnail image to select it. As the photo filled the screen, Simone could see that it was a picture of Neal and a friend at a party.

The friend had his arm draped across Neal's shoulder and both were laughing. She gasped as she studied the tanned, handsome face of Neal's friend.

Chim Chim pushed in closer. "What the—how does Neal know *Dr. Edwards?*"

Zoe peered over Simone's other shoulder. "That figures. Now we have another reason to dislike him."

"Scroll down farther," Chim Chim insisted.

Simone obliged, scrolling to the end of Neal's photo gallery. The only other personal photo was a selfie of Neal, Dr. Edwards, and Davina Spellman—Sabrina's owner—at an outdoor festival or event. Now that they knew Davina was dating Dr. Edwards, the photo didn't seem too suspicious—only further evidence of Neal and the doctor's friendship. Simone shrugged and pressed the button to return to Neal's home screen.

"What about his text messages?" Zoe asked. "There might be something damaging in them."

"Good idea." Simone tapped the icon to access Neal's text messages. "I know you're hiding *something*, Neal," she said, staring at the phone. "We just need to find it." Scrolling down, she saw Audrey's picture next to her name, indicating a group of text messages between Neal and their owner. She pressed on Audrey's picture to pull them up.

The most recent message was from Neal. It was dated Friday, the day they left on the cruise. The text read, *Pick you up at noon.* Audrey had simply replied with a *K* and a smiley face emoji. The messages prior to that were sent last Wednesday. *Two more days until our trip. Can't wait! I miss you,* read the text from Neal. The reply from Audrey said, *Miss U 2,* with a heart.

"Ugh!" Chim Chim said, reading over Simone's shoulder.

Simone felt like gagging herself. She continued reading through the messages, but nothing caught her interest. There were about forty messages in the group, indicating that Neal hadn't deleted anything in a while.

She exited out of the message thread. Scrolling down the list, she saw messages from Neal's sister, one labeled "Steve – Office," and a group of messages from "Ryan."

"That's Dr. Edwards's first name," Zoe said.

"Yeah, the photo looks like him. We should check them out," Simone said. She clicked on Dr. Edwards's photo, and the messages between them were displayed. There were more than thirty messages in the group, as in Audrey's.

Simone started reading the messages from Dr. Edwards. The most recent was dated the week before the cruise. Neal had texted, *Leaving on my cruise Friday. Need more Tranquilta for Audrey.* The reply from Dr. Edwards said, *She's still giving it to the old girl, huh? Good. I'll leave it at the front desk for you.* Neal responded, *Thx.* Then Dr. Edwards gave him a thumbs-up emoji.

"Hmph!" Zoe snorted behind her.

Simone looked over her shoulder. "We took care of that bottle, too. So don't you worry, Zoe." She gave a firm nod for emphasis and turned back to the phone. Most of the messages were harmless—planning after-work get-togethers and such. The oldest message in the thread was dated September, which was only a couple of months ago. She started reading.

I have that new veterinary drug I told you about, Dr. Edwards had texted. *It's called Tranquilta.*

Is it safe? Neal had asked.

More or less, Dr. Edwards answered. He'd added three emojis that were laughing and crying at the same time. *Does it matter? I know how much you LOVE animals.*

To that, Neal had responded, *LOL.* Then he'd added laughing emojis of his own. He followed that by texting, *Her stupid cats will be out of my way soon enough. Just need to convince her to give it to them.*

Dr. Edwards replied, *I'll see if I can help. The white coat usually gets people to listen.*

Thanks. I owe you, Neal responded.

Dr. Edwards ended the discussion with *NP.*

Simone was stunned. She knew this Neal guy was bad, but she hadn't realized just *how* bad. And she couldn't believe Audrey had been so easily brainwashed by him. There were no words for what she was feeling. She could only stare at Neal's phone.

For once, Chim Chim was speechless as well.

"Well, ladies," Zoe said, "it sounds like we have more than one enemy on our hands. We have our work cut out for us."

"Yes . . . we do," Simone said, regaining her speech. "And it's time to find out exactly who—and what—we're up against."

Simone sat in front of Audrey's computer as Chim Chim and Zoe took an afternoon nap. Her paws hovered over the keyboard. She could use a nap herself, but she had important work to do. She typed "Neal Schuler, Valencia Springs" into the search engine. The first item that popped up was a link to the website of the insurance company Neal worked for. Simone clicked on the link. An article welcoming new employees pulled up. She peered at the date. It was old, from seven years back. The story included a photo of five people standing outside the company's corporate office. A caption underneath listed the employees' names. Neal, the second from the right, squinted in the sun as he attempted a smile for the photographer. "Hmm." His face was more youthful—and he had more hair—but Simone recognized those beady eyes anywhere!

The second item on the list of search results was a link to a story in their local newspaper, the *Valencia Springs Banner*. It was dated three years ago. She clicked on the article's heading, *"Dispute over Dog Ends in Jail Time, Restraining Order."* The article contained no pictures, but she gasped as she read the story:

A neighborly dispute ends in violence as Valencia Springs resident loses temper and vandalizes personal property. Neal Schuler, 32, of Laurel Lane, was arrested Friday for inflicting damage upon his neighbor's car after a heated argument over the neighbor's dog. Schuler was released from jail on bond Monday morning, and a restraining order has been issued. He is due in court on May 23. Schuler's neighbor Aaron Smith was cited with violation of the leash law.

"Hmm. I'd say Neal has a *definite* temper problem." Simone shook her head.

The remaining links on the list were for web pages related to other people with the same name as Neal—or with last names that were similar. Simone sighed and hit the back arrow to return to the search screen. She typed "Ryan Edwards, Veterinarian" into the search box. This time, a larger list of websites popped up. She scrolled down, reading.

Another article from the *Valencia Springs Banner*, "*Valencia Springs Veterinarian Celebrates Grand Opening of New Clinic*," topped the list. Simone started with that one, clicking on the link with her mouse.

Veterinarian Dr. Ryan Edwards announces the grand opening this Saturday of his new state-of-the-art veterinary clinic on Orange Valley Road. This facility will offer laser surgery, digital imaging, and other cutting-edge diagnostic services, along with the personal patient care his customers have grown to love. Edwards first came to Valencia Springs five years ago after graduating from Auburn University College of Veterinary

Medicine. Opening his first clinic on Racine Street, he built a successful client base that soon outgrew his original facility. Mayor Linda Gardner will perform the ribbon-cutting ceremony for the new clinic on Saturday. Festivities start at 9:00 a.m. and will include prize giveaways, a "bouncy house" for the kids, pet photo opportunities, and refreshments for all.

"Hmph!" Simone snorted. She remembered Audrey dragging her sister to that event last year. If she and Chim Chim had been dogs, Audrey would have dragged them along, too. She cringed at the thought of being dressed in stupid costumes to pose for pet photos. She was very thankful to be a cat!

Simone clicked the back arrow and scrolled through the list of search results. The next link was to Action News 8 in Orlando, which had also covered the grand opening event. The remaining links related to Dr. Edwards were to his clinic's website and his social media pages.

She returned to the search box and typed in "Tranquilta, pet deaths." Many of the websites she had studied a few weeks back popped up in the list again, along with some additional news story links. She scrolled down the list, squinting at the tiny descriptions. Nothing seemed to stand out, so she clicked on the "2" at the bottom of the screen for the next page of search results.

An item on the second page caught her attention: *"Georgia Veterinarian Investigated for Multiple Pet Deaths after Prescribing Non-FDA-Approved Medicines."*

"Yikes!" Simone wasn't sure what a disgraced Georgia vet had to do with Tranquilta. She moved closer to the screen. "Oh." Below the link were the words "Missing: ~~Tranquilta~~." The search engine had included it because she'd entered "pet deaths." So it wasn't related at all. But still—the headline made her curious, so she clicked on the news article with her mouse.

The FDA's Office of Criminal Investigations confirmed Friday that a warrant was issued for the arrest of Sandy Springs, Georgia, veterinarian Dr. Michael Frazier. Frazier was charged with prescribing veterinary medicines that have not been approved by the FDA, resulting in five pet deaths in the Atlanta area. Frazier is now in custody, awaiting trial.

Simone knew that "FDA" was short for the Food and Drug Administration, a federal government agency that regulates the production of human food and medicines, along with medicines for pets. Going around the FDA was illegal—and reason enough for a veterinarian to get in trouble, even without deaths involved.

The news article was dated eight years ago. Simone studied the photo, which showed Dr. Frazier being led away in handcuffs. The men escorting him wore navy-blue jackets that bore the golden seal of the FDA-OCI. The photo showed only the back of the doctor, but Simone could tell he was young—in human years. He had short, reddish-brown hair and wore nice clothes. The handcuffs weren't a good fashion statement, though. Simone shook her head.

She clicked the back arrow and studied the article list again. *"Trial set for Sandy Springs' 'Doctor Death.'"* Her eyes widened as she selected the article.

Trial has been set in the case of Sandy Springs veterinarian, Dr. Michael Frazier—also known as "Doctor Death." Frazier is facing two years in prison and revocation of his veterinary license for prescribing medicines that have not been approved by the FDA. Authorities now confirm seven pet deaths in the Atlanta area from these illegal drugs, two of which were claimed to produce a "calming effect" by their manufacturer.

"Wow," Simone whispered. This Dr. Frazier must have been quite an immoral character! At least Tranquilta was FDA-approved. She shuddered. She'd hate to think what might have happened to Zoe if it hadn't been.

Simone exited the internet browser and powered down the computer with a sigh. She had hoped to dig up some dirt on both Neal *and* Dr. Edwards. But it appeared that the doc was as squeaky-clean as he claimed to be.

So why did she still have such a nagging feeling?

CHAPTER 13
Old Friends, New Problems

Chim Chim batted her favorite toy mouse around the Florida room as the sun made bright rectangles on the indoor-outdoor carpeting. Simone dozed on the glass-topped table, and Zoe napped nearby on the patio sofa. Chim Chim glanced over as her elderly housemate began to snore softly. She smiled, turning her attention back to her toy. She and Zoe had done a lot to improve their relationship over the past year. Chim Chim no longer thought of her as bossy and mean; the older cat had simply been through some bad times in her life. Chim Chim liked to think that Zoe thought of *her* a little more fondly now, too. She may have even earned the older cat's respect.

Chim Chim looked up as she heard the clicking of toenails on cement. A familiar golden retriever trotted up the sidewalk, his plumed tail joyfully beating the air. Humphrey approached the screen door, giving it a couple of raps with his front paw. Then he stood back to wait.

Chim Chim left her mouse and padded over to the screen door. "Hello, Humphrey," she greeted warmly. She rose on her back legs and hit the door latch with her paw. Then she nosed the door open to allow him to enter.

"Hello, Chim Chim," he said, grinning. Humphrey was *always* grinning—in fact, Chim Chim had never seen him in a bad mood. "Ladies." He nodded at Simone and Zoe.

Simone, now awake, stretched and jumped down from the table to join them. Zoe was slower in rising.

"Hi, Humphrey," Simone said. "What brings you out on this lazy afternoon?"

"I enjoy these autumn days," Humphrey said. "Not too hot—but not cold, either. It feels good on the joints."

"That it does," Zoe agreed, padding over to them. She gave her back legs a good stretch.

"So you're out for a stroll?" Chim Chim asked.

"Well, yes . . . and no," Humphrey answered. His grin faded, making him look more serious. The white fur around his mouth added to the effect, Chim Chim thought.

Humphrey cleared his throat. "I have a message for the ladies of Crime Busters," he began. "One of your former contacts, Pancho Ramirez, has some concerns. He's worried about his housemate, Lefty."

"I'd think things would have returned to normal, now that the petnappers are in jail and Lefty is back home," Simone said. "But from what I remember, Pancho was always worried about something."

"That's an understatement," Chim Chim agreed. An anxious Chihuahua was nothing new. "So, what seems to be the trouble now?"

"According to Pancho," Humphrey said, "Lefty's had some difficulty readjusting to normal life after his time spent captive. He described the old Lefty as being a daredevil and risk-taker. *Now* the poor guy is constantly nervous and afraid—even afraid to go outside and do his 'business.'"

"Well, outside *is* where he was abducted, so that's a reasonable fear," Simone said. "Hmm. He could be suffering from PTSD."

"PTSD?" Chim Chim asked, raising an eyebrow.

"Post-traumatic stress disorder," Simone explained. "It's a mental disorder that affects humans—most often soldiers—who experience traumatic events. I've seen several news programs on it, and they all say it can be very serious. PTSD can cause anxiety, fear, even nightmares."

"But you said *humans*," Chim Chim said. "Can animals get this disorder, too?"

"I hadn't heard of any animals having it," Simone said. She rubbed her chin. "But we *are* getting more and more of the medical conditions that affect humans."

"Yes, we are," Humphrey agreed.

Chim Chim shook her head. "This isn't good."

"No," Simone said. "We need to pay Pancho and Lefty a visit."

"Oh, really? *We?*" Chim Chim asked. She was still annoyed with Simone for excluding her from visiting Pancho last year, when Lefty was kidnapped. She hadn't seen either of the Chihuahuas in a while. Hector, their owner, wasn't one for strolling around the neighborhood.

"Yes, *we*," Simone said. "I'm sure Hector has relaxed a bit, now that the petnappers are behind bars. We won't have to be quite as careful."

"Okay, fine," Chim Chim conceded.

"Do you know what shift Hector is working this week?" Simone asked Humphrey.

"I'm not certain, but I can check."

"That would be great," Simone said. "Thank you."

"Thanks, dude," Chim Chim said. It was good to be friends with the "head dog" of the neighborhood—if Humphrey didn't know everything that was going on, he made it his business to find out.

"No problem," Humphrey said, his grin returning. "As always, the animal residents of Highland Oaks—myself included—appreciate all you do for us." He bowed slightly.

"It's our pleasure," Simone said. She smiled warmly. "Bye, Humphrey."

"Good-bye, ladies."

Chim Chim hit the latch and nosed the door open for him. She watched as he trotted down the sidewalk, his golden tail wagging behind him. "Do you really think Lefty might have this . . . PTSD?"

"It's very likely," Simone said. "Kidnapping is a traumatic experience—for animals *or* humans. I'll know more when I can speak with him in person and study his body language."

Chim Chim nodded.

"As soon as we hear from Humphrey, we'll plan our visit."

"Sounds good, boss," Chim Chim said. She returned to her toy mouse with a *squeak!*

Late Thursday morning, Chim Chim and Simone scampered through the grass to the bridge that spanned the canal behind their house. Chim Chim paused midway across, glancing down at the canal water. She was relieved to see that it was almost back to its normal level.

No traffic was about, so they trotted down Pine and turned left on Laurel Street. Humphrey had confirmed that Hector was working the day shift this week, so they were safe to visit Pancho and Lefty.

They approached the third house on the left, a neat white home with brick-red shutters. Chim Chim noticed that Hector's lawn was perfectly maintained—not a weed or tall blade of grass anywhere. If his yard had suffered any damage from the storm, it certainly didn't show it.

"Have you ever been inside Pancho and Lefty's house?" Simone asked, pausing at the edge of the Chihuahuas' driveway.

"I've talked to them in passing, out in the yard," Chim Chim said. "But no, I've never gone inside."

"Mmm. Their house is pretty plain, compared to ours. Hector's not much of a decorator since his wife died."

"Audrey's not much of a decorator herself," Chim Chim reminded her.

Simone laughed. "Yeah, I guess you're right." She glanced at Chim Chim. "You ready?"

"Let's do this."

They padded side by side down the driveway to the side entrance, which contained a small pet door at the bottom. At Simone's nod, Chim Chim stepped forward and gave the plastic flap a couple of raps with her front paw. She waited several seconds; then she knocked again.

"Who is it?" a timid voice asked.

"Chim Chim and Simone from Crime Busters," Chim Chim replied. "Is this Pancho?"

"No, it's Lefty."

"Hello, Lefty," Simone said, pushing in closer. "May we come in and talk?"

The Chihuahua's voice grew more hesitant. "Uh . . . sure. I guess so. Did I do something wrong?"

"No, of course not," Simone assured him. "We just wanted to check and see how you're doing since your return home." She turned to Chim Chim with one eyebrow raised.

"Definitely *not* normal," Chim Chim whispered, agreeing with Simone's unspoken thoughts.

"Oh, well, let me see if the pet door is locked," Lefty said. A small foot pushed through the hazy plastic flap. "Okay. You can, uh . . . come in."

Chim Chim waited as Simone pushed through the pet door first. Then she followed closely behind, stopping inside to survey her surroundings.

Wow, Chim Chim thought. Simone had said Hector's house was plain, but seeing was believing! There were no bright colors, no busy prints—not even an ounce of clutter. The kitchen was L-shaped, with nothing but a set of beige ceramic canisters and an empty dish rack on the counter—a far cry from the chaos of Audrey's house. Hector's furniture was simple, too: a leather couch, a worn recliner, a coffee table, and a modest television. All neutral colors, all boring. Chim Chim was starting to appreciate having a female owner—at least she had *some* fashion sense!

"Uh, Pancho's in there," Lefty said. He jerked his head toward the adjoining room.

"Thanks," Simone said with a warm smile.

Chim Chim followed Simone into the living room. Pancho lay on the leather couch, engrossed in a courtroom show on television. Hector must be the kind of owner who left the TV on for his pets while he was at work—Chim Chim had heard of people like that. Of course, being a cat, she had no need for added noise. If her favorite shows were on, she was perfectly capable of working a remote control.

"Hello, Pancho," Simone greeted. "You remember Chim Chim, don't you?"

Pancho looked down. His face immediately brightened as he recognized them. "Yes, of course! Hello, Simone." His short tail gave a friendly wag. "Hello, Chim Chim." Pancho and Lefty were both tan-colored Chihuahuas, with white on their undersides and muzzles. But unlike Lefty, whose ears were partly white, the inside of Pancho's ears was black.

Chim Chim smiled at the little Chihuahua. "Morning."

Lefty scampered past them. Chim Chim noticed that his tail—normally held slightly upward when he walked—was tucked downward, and he appeared to be trembling. He joined Pancho on the couch and lay down, watching them warily. *Very odd,* she thought—not odd for the breed of dog, but definitely odd for a daredevil like Lefty.

"So, how have you guys been doing?" Simone asked. She looked up at Lefty. "Isn't it great to be home?"

Lefty's eyes widened, as if he hadn't expected to be spoken to. "Me? Oh, yeah, sure. It's uh . . . great. Really great." He dropped his chin onto his paws and stared at the floor, as if he hoped the mere act would make him invisible.

Chim Chim sighed. She couldn't believe the transformation in him. "It's good to have you back, Lefty."

Lefty forced a hint of a smile and closed his eyes.

Pancho studied Lefty for a few seconds. He turned to Chim Chim and Simone, bewildered, and shook his head sadly.

Simone motioned to Pancho with a jerk of her head toward the kitchen. Then she gave Chim Chim a nod and padded out of the living room.

Chim Chim followed, waiting with Simone by the pet door. It was strange to see Pancho as the confident one of the pair and Lefty the timid one.

"Do you see what I mean?" Pancho whispered as he joined them. His brown eyes were grim.

"Yes," Simone said. "Yes, I do."

"That's definitely not the Lefty I know," Chim Chim said, frowning.

"How is he sleeping at night?" Simone asked. "Any nightmares?"

"Oh, he has terrible nightmares." Pancho trembled as if he'd experienced them himself. "He jerks and squirms and eventually cries out, waking everybody up."

"Has Hector noticed the change in his behavior?" Simone asked. "Apart from the nightmares?"

"Yes, he has," Pancho said. "Hector called today and made an appointment with the vet to get Lefty checked out again. I heard him telling the receptionist that he fears Lefty may have some internal injuries—from his captivity at the lab—that the state veterinarians missed."

"I agree that it's probably something internal—but not due to any physical injury," Simone said. "I believe he may have post-traumatic stress disorder."

"Like humans experience?" Pancho asked.

"Exactly," Simone said.

"But how would they treat an animal for something like that?" Chim Chim asked. "It's not as if they have *pet psychiatrists* listed in the phone book."

"No, but they do have experts in pet behavior—like that guy on TV," Simone said. "I don't know if they'd have one in Valencia Springs, though. Hector may have to take him to a bigger city, such as Orlando or Tampa."

"Maybe your vet can refer him to someone good," Chim Chim suggested.

"Yes," Simone agreed. "Be patient for now, Pancho. Let

us know what you find out about the vet visit. You can send word again through Humphrey."

"Okay. Thanks, ladies," Pancho said. He managed a meek smile. "It's reassuring to have friends."

"Anytime, dude," Chim Chim said. She placed a comforting paw on Pancho's shoulder. Then she turned and followed Simone through the pet door.

"Poor guy," Chim Chim said as they padded out to the street.

"Yeah, I'm worried about him," Simone said. "I'm curious to find out what the vet says."

"Me, too. I sure hope his vet isn't Dr. Edwards."

"Oh, no—that hadn't occurred to me," Simone said, stopping briefly in the street. "Well, for Lefty's sake, we'd better hope it isn't."

Chim Chim nodded. She followed Simone down Pine Street toward home.

CHAPTER 14
Croc Call

Something was bugging Simone. She woke before dawn with a nagging at her brain that forced out all chance of sleep. It demanded to be heard, and she had no choice but to listen. She let herself out quietly through the pet door and stepped through the soft, dewy grass up the hill to the narrow bridge. She did her best thinking when no one was around—especially Chim Chim—and the early morning stillness would provide some solitude.

Simone padded across the bridge and down Pine Street toward the back of the housing development. The streetlights remained on, but the eastern sky was beginning to turn a light gray, signaling that dawn was on its way. There were few cars out this early, and even fewer animals. She passed Spruce Street and then Laurel. Reaching Sycamore, she strolled down the footpath toward Lake Marion and the boat dock. She heard a car leaving on its way to work, but she kept her eyes on the structure ahead.

The boat dock, which doubled as a fishing pier, was built when Highland Oaks was in its early construction phase—or so Simone was told. That was ten years ago, so she hadn't been born yet. The only residents who remained from that time were Humphrey and his owner, Bill. Humphrey had been a mere pup then, but he still talked about that period with fond excitement.

Simone stepped across the weathered boards in the dark, careful not to get her paws caught between them. No one was out fishing at this early hour—which would've been highly unlikely in the summer. On muggy mornings from May through September, retired residents were out well before dawn with their lines extended. Now, in early November, the mornings were cooler and fewer people were about.

Simone soon reached the end of the dock. She sat on her haunches and gazed out upon the dark water. The air was quite still; no breeze had risen yet to coax the water into waves that would lap at the shoreline. She heard a soft noise as the water rippled before her. Looking down, she could make out the outline of an alligator's snout, back, and tail as it glided smoothly through the water. It was Calvin, Highland Oaks's oldest animal resident. He had lived in Lake Marion for over forty years. He'd also been their client during the Divinity Labs case. Crime Busters had helped clear his name of the petnapping claims—which had also helped to save his life.

Calvin coasted to a stop before the dock. He allowed his lower body to sink below the surface of the water, which enabled his head to rise slightly above it. "Hello, Simone."

"Hello, Calvin," Simone greeted warmly. His predatory teeth looked as sharp as ever, but she now knew there was nothing to fear. "It's nice to see you out cruising the lake."

"Yes. I'm finally feeling comfortable in my own surroundings again—thanks to you ladies at Crime Busters."

"All in a day's work," Simone assured him with a smile. "It was our pleasure to help."

"So tell me, Simone," Calvin began. "What are *you* doing out at this hour of the morning? I don't usually see you roaming about before dawn."

She furrowed her brows. "I know. I *should* be feeling comfortable myself—especially with no open Crime Busters cases right now. But something is keeping me from sleep."

"Any idea what might be bothering you, my dear?" Calvin asked in his clipped, British-sounding accent.

Simone sighed. "No—I mean, yes. Well, maybe. Something strange is going on around here."

Calvin waited politely, remaining afloat as she focused her thoughts.

"Several animals in our neighborhood have been displaying unusual behavior."

"Such as?" Calvin asked.

"Well, for starters, Jack—our Jack Russell neighbor—has been very sluggish and disoriented. He's usually so hyper, you have to hold him down to get a sentence out of him! Then there's Vervain . . ." She trailed off.

"Vervain?"

"Oh, sorry," Simone said. "Vervain is a German shepherd friend who helped us catch the petnappers last year. He's a great dog, but he's normally very gruff—and a bit scary—from a cat's perspective."

"How is this Vervain acting now?"

"Like a canine Romeo."

Calvin cocked his head slightly, as if waiting for an explanation.

"*Romeo* is a term humans use to describe someone who is lovable to the ladies," Simone explained. "The exact opposite of normal guard dog behavior."

"Hmm," Calvin said. "That is indeed puzzling. What about your housemates? Are any of *them* acting strangely?"

"No, but . . ." Simone paused. "I don't know if this is related at all, but we've had a different sort of trouble at home. My older housemate, Zoe, has been very sick, and as a result, has spent a lot of time at the vet's office."

"Had she been anywhere prior to her illness? Any place she might have gotten into something?"

"No," Simone said, shaking her head as she thought back. "She hasn't been anywhere at all—except the vet's office. She went for her annual visit a couple of days before she started getting sick."

"Then have you considered the possibility that her *illness* is the result?" Calvin asked. "Not the vet visit?"

"It has definitely crossed my mind," Simone said.

"I find that when trying to solve a puzzle," Calvin suggested, "it helps to trace your steps back to the time *before* the problem occurred. Then you examine each and every thing leading up to it—to see if any of those changes might have caused the situation. It may be something you completely overlooked the first time."

"Yeah, you're right," Simone agreed. "I think I knew that, too—deep down—but I was refusing to listen to my own inner wisdom."

"Now, Simone," Calvin admonished. "An animal's natural instinct is how we've survived on this planet for so many thousands of years. Never disregard that voice inside of you."

"I won't, Calvin." She gave him a warm smile. "Thanks."

"You're very welcome," Calvin said. "I'm simply returning the favor. It was good seeing you again."

Simone rose to leave. "You too, my friend. Take care." She watched as Calvin let his snout sink below the water and his abdomen rise up. He turned in a fluid motion and swam off with a powerful thrust of his rear leg muscles, his tail gliding in an S-shaped pattern.

Simone sauntered back down the dock toward the footpath. She felt a little better, having shared her concerns with another living being. It also helped to have her instincts confirmed. Maybe now she could get some sleep. And then she would get to the bottom of this!

That afternoon, as the sun made its journey toward the western horizon, Simone padded into the kitchen. She had questions, and her friend Caleb—a K-9 with the Valencia

Springs Police Department—could usually help find the answers. It was shortly after 4:00 p.m., so Caleb and his handler might be at the station, depending on which shift they were working that week. Caleb and John no longer worked out on patrol, since John's promotion to detective two years ago. But as they'd been together for seven years, Caleb had been allowed to remain with John.

Simone leaped upon the kitchen counter and gently pushed the telephone off its cradle. Then she nudged it over so that the mouthpiece was facing up. She punched in the direct number to John Pearson's desk at the Valencia Springs Police Department with her paw and leaned close to the earpiece. She let it ring twice and was about to hang up—the Crime Busters secret code—when a human voice promptly answered.

"Detective Pearson."

Simone's breath drew in sharply as she hurriedly clicked the red call-end button. John didn't normally answer the phone so quickly! She exhaled slowly. Luckily, Audrey had an unlisted phone number, so it wouldn't show on John's caller ID. But now Caleb would have no way of knowing she had called. *Darn.* She left the phone next to its cradle and wandered into the living room.

Chim Chim was sprawled on the couch, enjoying a nature show on television. She glanced over as Simone joined her. "Problems?"

"Sort of. I'm trying to reach Caleb, but John answered before I could do our two-ring code. I'll have to try again in a few minutes."

"Audrey will be home at 4:30," Chim Chim pointed out.

"I know," Simone said with a sigh. She rested her chin on her forepaws and tried to concentrate on the program, but the show was a repeat. At the commercial break, she padded back into the kitchen. She leaped once more upon the counter and redialed John's number.

This time no one picked up the phone, so Simone hung up after the second ring. She dialed the number again, hoping her friend hadn't gone home for the day.

"Hello?" answered a hoarse whisper of a voice.

"Caleb?"

"Simone?"

"Yeah, it's me," Simone replied. "Why are you whispering?"

"John's gone to the restroom, but he'll be back any minute," Caleb said. "What's up?"

"I need you to check into something for me. Are you guys about to head home, or are you on late shift this week?"

"We're on second. Our shift ends at midnight."

"Good," Simone said. "Potty break at the usual time?"

"You betcha."

"I'll meet you in the alley then, my friend."

"Okay, Simone," Caleb said. "Be careful."

"I will, Caleb. Bye."

"Bye," he whispered, hanging up quickly.

Simone pressed the call-end button and nudged the phone back onto its receiver. She jumped down and rejoined Chim Chim in the living room.

"I'm going to pay Caleb a visit at the station tonight. I have some things I want him to check into for me."

Chim Chim nodded. "Do you want me to go with you?"

"No, I'll be fine. Two cats out wandering at night might draw the attention of Animal Control."

"Yeah, you're right," Chim Chim agreed. "But still, if you need me . . ."

"Thanks, little buddy." Simone smiled as she stretched out beside Chim Chim on the couch. She reached for the TV remote with a sigh—she *hated* waiting.

Simone padded toward the front entrance of the Valencia Springs police station shortly before 8:00 p.m. The cement sidewalk felt cool beneath her paws as she passed the large glass windows that encased the lobby. No humans sat in the dingy orange plastic seats tonight, and no one waited in front of the service counter. The only person in sight was a lone man who sat behind the counter, his eyes glued to a computer screen. The light from the monitor reflected off his glasses, turning his face a bluish-white.

Simone continued past the lobby, glancing up as the traffic light at the end of the block clicked to green. Other than that, the streets were pretty quiet—most of the businesses downtown had closed by 6:00 p.m. She rounded the building and padded into the alley behind the police station. With no crickets singing on this cool night, the alley was as silent as the streets.

Simone knew from prior visits that Caleb was let out for a potty break halfway through John's work shift. So she settled next to the trash cans to wait.

Twenty minutes later, the back door opened to let a trim red-and-black German shepherd outside. "Don't wander off, Caleb," said a kindly voice. The door swung shut behind him.

Simone stepped out of the shadows. She noticed her white fur appeared pale yellow in the dim light by the back door.

The K-9 sniffed the air. "Evening, Simone," he said in a raspy voice. "It's been a while." He smiled, showing his sharp, white teeth.

"Evening, Caleb," Simone said warmly. "I know . . . I'm sorry. It's hard to catch you now that you two work mostly days. I actually called twice earlier, but John answered the first time, so I hung up."

"Oh, that was you?" Caleb laughed. "Yeah, he got a little irritated about it."

"I'm sorry."

"No worries," Caleb said. "So, to what do I owe this visit? Are you working a big case?" he asked eagerly.

"Kind of. Not a *paid* case, but still . . . a puzzle I need to solve. What do you know about Dr. Ryan Edwards?"

"The veterinarian? A little," Caleb said. "He's my vet, so I see him two or three times a year—but John doesn't hang out with him socially, if that's what you mean."

"Hmph! You're lucky."

Caleb cocked his head.

"I have a deep suspicion that Dr. Edwards isn't as respectable as he claims to be," Simone said. "I think he's hiding something—maybe something big." She paused. "He's prescribing questionable drugs for a member of my household, and I don't think these medicines are safe."

"Wow—not good," Caleb said. "You want me to run his name through the police database?"

"Could you, please?" Simone asked, giving him a sweet smile. "And one more thing—see what you can find out about a guy named Neal Schuler: S-c-h-u-l-e-r. He's my owner's new beady-eyed boyfriend, and he's behind this push to drug my housemate. Apparently he and Dr. Edwards are pals."

"Certainly," Caleb growled. "If there's one thing I don't like, it's humans who abuse animals."

"Me, either," Simone said. "I owe you big time, my friend."

"It's no problem. I'll see what I can find out."

"Thanks, Caleb," Simone purred. If she were human, she'd have given him a big hug!

CHAPTER 15

Out of Left Field

Chim Chim licked a glossy black paw and raised her chin to receive the cool breeze that blew through the Florida room's screened walls. She loved, loved, *loved* the dry air of fall! She twisted to clean a difficult spot on her lower back, then paused, cocking her head toward the street. A faint *click, click, click* greeted her ears.

Chim Chim turned, looking for Simone, but her house-mate was nowhere to be seen. Her ears perked as the clicking noise grew louder. Leaping down from the table, she padded over to the screened window by the pet door and peered out. Sure enough, a tiny form scurried into view. She realized the clicking noise was from tiny dog toenails—and that tiny dog appeared to be a Chihuahua. "Uh, Simone?" she cried, looking over her shoulder. "Simone!"

Simone's furry face poked through the pet door from the kitchen. "What is it, Chim Chim?"

"Someone's coming this way, and they seem to be in

a hurry." Chim Chim squinted at the approaching dog. "I think it's Pancho."

"Pancho? What on earth would he be doing way over here?" Simone appeared beside Chim Chim, shaking her head.

"You've got me." Chim Chim shrugged. "But Hector will be livid if he finds out."

She and Simone stared at the tiny Chihuahua as it approached.

Pancho paused at the edge of their sidewalk, his eyes darting to the driveway and back. He looked uncertain.

"It's okay, Pancho," Simone called out. "Come to the pet door—it's at the end of the sidewalk, next to the human door."

Pancho jerked, startled at the sound of Simone's voice. His ears cocked in their direction. "Oh, sure, Simone. I see you now." He hurried down the sidewalk toward them.

"That's it," Simone encouraged. "Push through—it's unlocked."

Chim Chim and Simone stepped back to give Pancho room to come through. His tan head appeared first, eyes bulging. Then he stepped daintily through the plastic frame. The pet door swung back and forth, swatting him on the behind. He jumped away with a startled *yelp!*

Chim Chim forced herself not to giggle as she glanced at her housemate. Simone chewed her lower lip in an apparent effort to do the same.

"So, what are you doing on this side of the neighborhood, Pancho?" Simone asked. She raised an eyebrow.

"Alone, at that."

Pancho took a deep breath, which appeared to help his trembling. "It's Lefty. Something's very wrong, and I couldn't wait for Humphrey to stop by."

"Lefty?" Simone asked. Her brow furrowed. "But I thought Hector took him to the vet for treatment."

"Yes, he did. But that's the problem."

"What do you mean?" Chim Chim asked. "Wasn't the vet able to help him?"

"No, not really," Pancho said. He turned to Simone. "The vet did diagnose him with that PTSD you told us about, and he prescribed Lefty some medicine." Pancho sighed. "But now Lefty's acting even stranger."

"Stranger how?" Simone asked.

"Well, for starters, he sleeps *all* the time," Pancho said, "and he doesn't eat. When I try to talk to him, he just stares at me with a glazed look. He doesn't respond at all."

"That's not good," Simone said, rubbing her chin.

"Not good at all," Chim Chim agreed. "I thought doctors were supposed to make people and animals *better*."

"Yeah, well . . . apparently that's not the case around here," Simone said. She looked thoughtful for a moment. "Pancho?"

"Yes, Simone?"

"I need you to do something for me."

"Um, sure." Pancho began to tremble again. "Wh—what is it?"

"I need you to go home and find the medication bottle that the vet sent home with Lefty."

"Medication?" Pancho's eyes bulged. "You mean, go through Hector's cabinets?" His trembling worsened to a shaking.

"It's okay, Pancho," Chim Chim said. *Poor little guy!* "You'll be fine. Just make sure you put everything back before Hector comes home, and he won't notice a thing."

"Chim Chim's right," Simone said. "Hector loves you. He'd never do anything to harm you or Lefty—at least not knowingly."

"Oh, I know," Pancho said. "He has a big heart. But his 'bark' can be so much worse than his bite." He gave a meek smile.

Simone patted him on the shoulder. "Everything will be fine. But I need you to find out what kind of medication Lefty is on. Then I can research it and see if his behavior is a side effect."

"Okay," Pancho said timidly.

"And get back to us as soon as you can," Chim Chim added.

"Yes," Simone agreed. "Do you know how to use a telephone?"

"Yes . . . I think so. I've watched Hector use it many times—it can't be that hard."

"It's not," Simone said. "Hold on a second." She dashed over to the step and bolted through the inner pet door.

Pancho turned to Chim Chim with a puzzled look, his brow furrowing.

"I . . . I'm not sure." Chim Chim shrugged. Even after five years together, she still couldn't read Simone's mind.

"But she'll be right back."

Simone appeared seconds later, shoving back through the pet door from the kitchen. She carried an ink pen in her mouth, which she dropped onto the carpet. "Hold up a paw, Pancho," she instructed. "I'd give you one of our business cards, but I ran out of the card stock to print them on. So we're going to try this instead." She held the pen down with a front paw while pulling the lid off with her teeth. She spit it out and waited for Pancho.

The Chihuahua lifted his right forepaw, shifting his weight to keep his balance.

Simone took the pen in her left forepaw and curled her toe pads around it, squeezing tightly. She wrote a number, *555-1212*, on the smooth flesh of Pancho's paw pad. Then she blew on it to dry.

Pancho staggered slightly and shifted his weight again.

"Okay, that should be dry enough. You can put it down now, Pancho."

The little dog obliged. He looked at Simone questioningly.

"I wrote our phone number on your paw, so don't lift it up in front of Hector. Crime Busters has a secret code for the telephone: let it ring twice, then hang up and call right back. That lets us know the call's for us—not Audrey. Can you remember that?"

"Yes, I think I can."

"You'll need to call before 4:30 p.m., or else Audrey will be home," Chim Chim added.

"That's right," Simone agreed. "But if you forget—or the number accidentally gets washed off—you can always send word through Humphrey."

"Don't worry. I won't get it wet," Pancho assured them. He took a step toward the pet door, then turned back. "Thanks, ladies. I don't know what I'd do without you." His large brown eyes brimmed with tears.

Chim Chim padded Pancho on the shoulder. "We're here for you, dude."

Pancho nodded, then pushed through the pet door and out to the sidewalk. The *click, click click* of his toenails grew fainter as he scurried down the street.

"Lefty doesn't sound good," Chim Chim said.

"No, he doesn't," Simone agreed. "I was hoping the vet could help his PTSD, but it sounds like he only made things worse."

Chim Chim nodded silently. She hoped that, for Lefty's sake, they could figure something out—before it was too late.

Chim Chim wandered into the kitchen that evening as Audrey rushed around preparing dinner. Her feline brows knit together as she studied her empty food bowl. The rumble in her belly reminded her that she hadn't been fed.

Audrey looked over as she placed a pot on the stove. "Hungry, Chim Chim? I guess I forgot to feed you, huh?" She laughed, tapping her forehead with the palm of her hand.

Forgot, indeed! Chim Chim felt that pet feeding times should be a priority on Audrey's to-do list.

Audrey pulled the dry kibble container from the pet supply cabinet and filled Chim Chim's bowl. She filled Zoe's next and paused, hovering over Simone's bowl. Then she turned and strode back to the cabinet.

"Well, that was weird," Simone commented as she joined Chim Chim.

"Yeah—maybe she's putting you on a diet," Chim Chim suggested. "I *have* noticed a couple of extra pounds in your rear compartment!" She dissolved into peals of laughter.

Simone narrowed her eyes. "Very funny."

"Maybe Audrey's developing Alzheimer's?" Zoe suggested, padding into the kitchen. "She's been quite forgetful lately."

"I think that only affects *elderly* humans," Simone said.

Zoe shrugged, grabbing a mouthful of kibble.

Chim Chim's laughter ended abruptly as Audrey grabbed a medicine bottle from the basket on the pet supply cabinet. Her owner studied the label briefly. Then she unscrewed the lid and dumped a tiny white pill into the palm of her hand. Searching through the supply drawer, Audrey pulled out a small plastic-and-rubber pill shooter.

"Oh, no!" Chim Chim cried. "Zoe, *run!*"

Zoe obliged by spitting out her kibble and dashing down the hallway toward Audrey's bedroom.

"Zoe? What the—" Audrey's eyes widened in surprise. "Well, never mind." She turned toward Chim Chim and Simone. "Come here, baby."

Chim Chim's heart beat rapidly in alarm. "Which 'baby' is she talking to?"

"I'm not sure, but we'd better beat it!" Simone exclaimed.

Chim Chim bolted. She was halfway to the pet door when she realized Simone wasn't behind her. She gave a heavy sigh as she turned and trudged back.

Simone remained crouched by the food bowls, held in place by Audrey's knees. Their owner attempted to pry Simone's mouth open with one hand, while holding the pill shooter between the index and middle fingers of her other one.

Chim Chim tried to come up with a plan. Should she bite her human in the ankle? Should she trip Audrey, as she'd done Neal?

She could tell that Simone had clenched her jaws in an attempt to thwart their owner, but the effort was useless. Audrey finally forced the rubber end of the plastic pill shooter between Simone's teeth.

"Simone! Listen to me!" Chim Chim urged. "You've got to hold it in your mouth—*don't* swallow it! You can spit it out later, but let her believe she got the pill down your throat."

Audrey pressed on the end of the pill shooter with her thumb, expelling the pill into Simone's mouth. Then she dropped the device, immediately rubbing Simone's throat to force the cat to swallow.

"Hold it, Simone! Don't swallow!!" Chim Chim cried.

"There," Audrey said. She seemed satisfied as the muscles in Simone's throat contracted. "Sorry, baby." She rubbed the top of Simone's head. "It will all be worth it—you'll see." She climbed to her feet and filled Simone's food bowl. Then she wandered off to finish cooking.

Chim Chim moved closer to Simone, her brows furrowing anxiously.

Simone remained frozen in place, her muscles still tensed. She didn't speak, nor did she move.

Chim Chim was starting to worry. "Simone?" she asked softly. "Are you okay? Did you swallow the pill?"

After a couple seconds of silence, Simone uttered one word through clenched teeth. "Fine." She shook her head vigorously side to side.

"Yeah—don't try to talk," Chim Chim said.

Simone nodded. She padded quickly to the pet door and pushed through it.

Chim Chim followed, joining Simone in front of the marine print patio sofa. Mimicking her housemate, Chim Chim cocked her ears toward the house and listened intently. She heard the faint clacking of dishes and banging of pots, but no footsteps. Audrey didn't appear to be following them.

Satisfied, Simone spit the pill out on the indoor-outdoor carpeting and pushed it deep under the couch with her paw. "There—she won't find that for a while." She grimaced, sticking out her tongue.

Chim Chim figured it tasted bad—medicine always did. "What do you think it was?"

"My guess would be Tranquilta," Simone replied. "But I have no earthly idea why. I'm not anxious . . . or hyperactive."

"I'm sure it has something to do with that beady-eyed human!" Chim Chim declared with a snort. She narrowed her eyes as the muffled sound of singing reached their ears.

"Well, I'm sure this won't be her last attempt," Simone said, frowning. "And if Neal is behind this, I fear *none* of us will be safe."

Chim Chim swallowed hard.

CHAPTER 16
Repeat Offender

The insistent ringing of the telephone woke Simone from her nap for the second time that day. Pancho had called that morning, and his news was worse than Simone had feared: his vet had not only prescribed Lefty a medicine with side effects—he'd prescribed *Tranquilta!* She wasn't surprised to find out that their vet was Dr. Edwards. Apparently all the humans in Valencia Springs had fallen for his glamorous image.

She stretched, still feeling groggy.

Ring! The second ring startled her fully awake. It was followed by silence, so Simone jumped down and dashed through the pet door to wait in the kitchen. *Ring!* She leaped onto the countertop and nudged the phone from its receiver, pressing the green button with her paw.

"Hello?"

"Simone," greeted the raspy voice on the other end.

Simone smiled. "Hello, Caleb. What did you find out for me?"

"Not much on dear Dr. Edwards, I'm afraid," Caleb replied. "He appears to have been a model citizen. Of course, I only went back eight years. But he's pretty young, right?"

"I think so. Well . . ." Simone paused, rubbing her chin. "I'm not good with humans, but I'd say he's slightly older than Audrey. Maybe mid-thirties?"

Simone heard clicking noises in the background.

"The internet says that veterinarians have to go to school for eight years," Caleb said. "Then most work as interns for a year or two after graduation. Dr. Edwards started his practice here six years ago—so that sounds about right."

"Yes, it does."

"I can do a more extensive search if you want me to," Caleb offered. "But I'd have to have his fingerprints. Then I could run them through the FBI database and see if he's been in trouble in any other states."

"Great idea! I'll try to get them for you."

"Sounds good," Caleb said. "Hey, listen—I did find something on your owner's boyfriend, though."

"Really?" Simone grew excited. She felt her heartbeat quicken. "What?"

"Apparently, he got himself in a bit of hot water a few years back," Caleb said. "Lost his temper and vandalized his neighbor's car."

"Yeah, I read about that on the internet. Can you fax me over the police report?"

"Absolutely."

"Anything else on him?" she asked, still hopeful.

"Not a thing—sorry."

Simone sighed. "It's okay. Thanks for your help, Caleb. I—"

"You 'owe me'—I know." Caleb laughed. "Someday you'll get to pay me back."

"You're right. I will." Simone smiled. "Take care, my friend."

"You, too."

Simone clicked the red button to end the call and padded down the hall to Audrey's office. She sprang onto Audrey's desk as the fax machine began to ring and waited patiently for the report to print. When it was finished, she grasped the page in her jaws and laid it flat to read. "Yep. Definitely Neal." She gave a snort. "I'd recognize those beady eyes anywhere." She filed the paper in the back of the lowest file cabinet drawer—where she hid all their Crime Busters files.

She sauntered out to the patio table, where her little buddy lay sleeping. "Chim Chim." Simone watched as Chim Chim's ear twitched in her sleep. "Chim Chim!" Still no response. She gave a deep sigh and leaped onto the table beside Chim Chim, leaning down close to her face. "*Chim!*" she hissed, nudging her with a paw.

Chim Chim jerked back with a sharp intake of breath, her eyes wide. They narrowed as they focused on her housemate's face. "Simone!" She let out her breath in a rush. "Don't do that to me! You know I'm a deep sleeper."

Simone chuckled. "Sorry, little pal. But that was my *third* attempt." She backed away to give Chim Chim time to awaken—it was only polite. She padded over to the patio sofa, where Zoe lay watching intently.

Chim Chim stretched and stretched again. Then she gave an exaggerated sigh and jumped down from the table, wandering over to join them. "So what's this all about?" she grumbled. "Why did you so rudely interrupt my nap?"

Simone exchanged a knowing glance with Zoe and smiled. "I have my reasons, drama princess. Do you want to hear them?"

"Sure." Chim Chim climbed onto a marine-print patio chair that matched the sofa. She lay facing Simone, peering down her nose for dramatic effect.

"Okay." Simone glanced from Zoe to Chim Chim. "I just got a call from Caleb, and he wasn't able to find anything on Dr. Edwards."

"Nothing?" Chim Chim asked. "Not even a parking ticket?"

"Sadly, no," Simone said. "But he did fax over confirmation of Neal's arrest for destruction of property that I dug up."

"Sounds like Audrey's boyfriend isn't such a model citizen," Zoe said.

"Definitely not." Simone shook her head. "Caleb did suggest, though, that if we could get our paws on Dr. Edwards's fingerprints, he could do an interstate search on him."

"Good idea," Zoe said, nodding. "I didn't think of that."

"Neither did I," Simone said. "But no worries—we can work on it today."

"Work on it how?" Chim Chim asked, narrowing her eyes. "You're not going to use me as bait again, are you?"

"No, little buddy," Simone assured her. "I promised I'd never do that again—and I meant it." She gave a firm nod. "I think the best place to obtain his fingerprints would either be at his office, or . . . at his *girlfriend's* house." She emphasized the last word, wiggling her eyebrows.

"Oh, yeah," Chim Chim said with a smirk. "Sabrina's owner is Dr. Frankenstein's girlfriend." She stretched her forepaws out before her. "I don't know about you ladies, but I have no desire to go to Dr. Edwards's clinic."

"Nor do I!" Zoe exclaimed.

"Don't worry, Zoe—we're not going anywhere near his clinic," Simone assured her. She turned to her younger housemate. "But *you* are going to accompany me to Sabrina's house in a few minutes."

"I am?" Startled, Chim Chim sat upright. "Okay. Let me, um . . . stop by the litter box first."

Simone chuckled, giving Zoe another knowing look. "Take your time."

Simone and Chim Chim trotted across the bridge, heading toward the Spellman residence. The sky was laced with high, wispy clouds that prevented the sun from heating the pavement. So they were able to remain on the street.

"Does Sabrina know we're coming?" Chim Chim asked.

"No—I didn't have her owner's telephone number. It will be fine, though."

Chim Chim nodded.

They slowed their pace as they neared the 300 block of Pine Street. Simone surveyed the surroundings as they approached the large tan stucco house with gray trim. Davina—Sabrina's owner—worked as an advertising executive, which meant she would be at work during normal daytime hours. The neighboring driveways were empty, and no humans were about. So she and Chim Chim seemed safe from prying eyes.

They padded down Sabrina's driveway, taking the sidewalk up to the main entrance of the house. Noting the absence of a pet door, Simone approached the front door hesitantly.

"What now?" Chim Chim asked.

"I'm not sure," Simone said. "There may be a pet door in back. Let me see if I can get Sabrina's attention." She bunched her leg muscles and sprang toward the doorbell button, tapping it with a front paw. Landing on her haunches, she scooted back to wait as a melodic chime pattern sounded inside the house.

A couple of seconds later, a small furry face poked through the sheer curtains covering the narrow window that framed the door. Sabrina's face brightened as she recognized them. "Simone! Chim Chim!" Her voice was muffled through the glass—to Simone it sounded more like "Mi-mone" and "She-She."

Simone stepped closer, raising her voice so the little dog could hear. "Sabrina, do you have a pet door? Or any way to get out?"

Sabrina jerked her tan head toward the driveway. "Wound pack," she said. "Wound pack."

Chim Chim giggled. "I guess she wants us to go around back."

Simone smiled. "I'd say you're right." She turned back to Sabrina. "Okay, we'll meet you there."

Simone gave Chim Chim a nod as the Yorkie dog's face disappeared from view. She and Chim Chim padded back down the sidewalk and crossed the driveway, stepping off into the perfectly manicured St. Augustine grass. They rounded the house, stopping at a chain-link fence that enclosed the backyard.

"Uh-oh." Chim Chim studied the fence. "Should we jump it?"

"Yeah, I guess," Simone said, frowning. "Go ahead—give it a shot."

Chim Chim bunched her rear leg muscles and sprang easily over the four-foot fence.

Simone, who wasn't as small—or as young—as Chim Chim, eyed a nearby tree instead. She could jump the fence if she *had* to—she'd been known to clear six-foot fences in her day—but why make things harder than necessary?

Chim Chim glanced from Simone to the tree and laughed. "Suit yourself, Grandma."

Simone made a face at Chim Chim. She studied the tree, which grew right beside the chain-link fence. It was a large oak with long branches that swept over into Sabrina's yard. Simone backed away a couple of feet, then burst forward and shot up the tree. Her front claws made clicking noises as they sank into the thick bark. When she'd climbed high enough to clear the fence, she wiggled around the girth of the trunk and dropped softly into the grass beside Chim Chim. She smirked at her little pal and strode off, heading toward a large cement patio at the back of the house.

Simone passed wicker patio furniture with hunter green cushions positioned near a shiny new silver grill. She figured Davina must have lots of friends over for cookouts. She eyed a set of French doors on the back wall of the house. Next to it was a small square dog door. Simone padded toward it.

Sabrina's furry head poked through the small flap. "Simone! Chim Chim! Come on in." She smiled, showing her tiny sharp teeth, and disappeared inside.

Simone glanced behind her at Chim Chim. "Coming?"

"I wouldn't miss it."

Simone pushed headfirst through the small pet door and stepped aside to make room for Chim Chim. Her eyes widened as her gaze traveled the room. Sabrina's owner apparently made a lot of money! A large cream-colored leather sectional sofa dominated the living room floor in front of a seventy-inch flat-screen television set. A glass-topped coffee table with metal pineapple-shaped feet rested on a fluffy white rug in front of the sectional. Decorative floor lamps stood to each side.

Beyond the living room, a spacious kitchen equipped with expensive modern appliances opened into a large dining area. A mahogany table that seated eight was set with formal place settings. Simone whistled through her front teeth. *Nice!*

"Ditto," Chim Chim agreed. "Audrey sure couldn't afford this."

Simone shook her head. "No way."

Sabrina laughed—a high, bell-like sound that enchanted the ears. "Oh, you guys are silly. It's not *that* fancy."

"Maybe not to *you*, but it's definitely over *our* owner's pay grade," Simone said. "Does Davina even allow you on the furniture?"

"Certainly," Sabrina said. The little Yorkie jerked her head toward the couch, the pink bows jiggling at her ears. "See the towel on the far end of the couch? That's where I sit."

"Oh," Simone said, nodding. "Of course." She smiled. "Sabrina, we have a favor to ask of you."

Sabrina cocked her head. "Sure, Simone. What is it?"

"We need you to get something for us the next time Dr. Edwards comes over."

"Okay," Sabrina said slowly, her tiny brows furrowing. "But he doesn't come over every day."

"That's fine," Simone said. "We have time."

The Yorkie looked at them expectantly.

"We need you to sneak something that Dr. Franken—I

mean, Dr. Edwards touches," Chim Chim said. "Like a glass, or maybe a fork or spoon."

"Yes," Simone said. "Something that has his fingerprints on it."

"But why do you need that?" Sabrina asked.

"A friend of mine at the police station is going to run his prints for me," Simone explained. She took a deep breath. She didn't want to scare Sabrina, but she didn't want to lie to her, either. "We suspect that Dr. Edwards may be a bad man, and this is the only way to do a thorough background check on him."

"Oh." Sabrina grew silent, studying her pink-painted toenails. She looked up suddenly, her eyes widening. "You don't think *Davina's* bad, too, do you?" she asked in a small voice. She started to tremble.

"No—no, of course not," Simone assured her. "I'd say the only thing Davina's guilty of is poor taste in boyfriends."

Chim Chim snorted. "You've got *that* right."

Simone turned to Chim Chim with a raised eyebrow, causing Chim Chim to shrug.

Sabrina nodded her head. She seemed noticeably calmer.

"If you can get one of these items," Simone continued, "it might also help us find out what's going on with the pets around here. Many of them are acting strangely, and the common denominator—the link—to all of them is Dr. Edwards."

"Sure, Simone," Sabrina said. "But, um . . . I'm not able to leave, so how would I get it to you?"

"We'll come pick it up," Simone said. "You can send word through Humphrey when Davina takes you for a walk. Or you can call us—if you know how to use a telephone."

Sabrina brightened again, showing her tiny teeth. "I can use a phone!"

"Perfect." Simone nodded at Chim Chim. She gave Sabrina a grin as Chim Chim darted off to find a pen. "Hold up your paw."

CHAPTER 17

Out of Focus

Chim Chim awoke to the harsh sound of Audrey's alarm. *Beep! Beep! Beep!* She shoved her head under the spare pillow to muffle the noise as her owner reached out an arm to silence the shrill noise. Ten minutes later, she was rudely snatched from her pleasant dreams again. *Beep! Beep! Beep!* Audrey silenced the alarm again with another smack.

"Aargh! Why does she *always* have to hit the snooze button?" Chim Chim protested as she drew her head out from under the pillow. Neither of her housemates responded. She rose up and glanced around the bedroom. Zoe was missing from her usual spot on the carpet. But Simone was curled up at the foot of the bed, fast asleep.

Chim Chim watched as Audrey swung her feet to the floor and pulled herself up to a sitting position with a groan. After a couple of minutes, her owner reached over and turned off the alarm. Then she rose to her feet with another groan and stumbled down the hall toward the kitchen.

Chim Chim stretched her front leg muscles, then her back ones. She padded across the blanket to Simone and gave her a nudge. "Wake up—it's time for breakfast." She waited for a response, but the older cat continued to sleep. The softest of snores reached Chim Chim's ears.

She nudged her housemate again. "Simone. Wake up!" She gave Simone a couple of taps on the shoulder for good measure.

Simone's ear twitched as she started to stir.

Chim Chim gave a sigh of impatience. "Breakfast!" she said again.

Simone opened one eye. "Yes, Chim?"

"It's time for breakfast. Come on!"

"Oh, I'm not very hungry. I'm going to sleep a little longer." Simone shut her eyes again and returned to sleep. A smile spread across her furry white face.

Chim Chim furrowed her brows. "Suit yourself!" she exclaimed, jumping down from the bed. She didn't know what was wrong with Simone, but *she* wasn't missing out on a good meal! She padded down the hall to the kitchen.

Zoe was already eating breakfast. She paused, looking up as Chim Chim approached. "Where's Simone?"

"Sleeping," Chim Chim replied. "I couldn't get her up."

"Well, that's unusual," Zoe said with a frown. "She's usually the first one to the kitchen in the morning."

"Oh, yeah . . ." Chim Chim trailed off. "You're right." Zoe *was* right—Simone always beat her to breakfast. Could her pal be sick? Chim Chim started on her own meal. If Simone wasn't up before she finished eating, she'd go check on her.

Audrey stopped on her way through the kitchen and studied Simone's untouched food bowl. "Hmm. That's weird." She turned and strode out of the kitchen.

Chim Chim's brow furrowed. She glanced at Zoe.

"She's probably going to check on Simone," Zoe said.

Chim Chim nodded. She was sure their owner had things handled. When she'd finished her breakfast, Chim Chim pushed through the pet door and out to the Florida room. She leaped up onto the glass-topped patio table and began her cleanup.

An hour later, Audrey opened the sliding glass door and poked her head into the Florida room. "Hmm." She frowned as she looked around. "Simone must still be sleeping. Well, I'll see you girls later."

Chim Chim watched as Audrey slid the door shut and disappeared into the kitchen. She could hear the faint jingle of car keys, followed by the slam of a door and the loud clanging of the metal garage door. She guessed she had better check on Simone herself—Audrey didn't seem to be doing a good job at it.

Chim Chim jumped down and pushed through the inner pet door. She was surprised to see Simone standing over her food bowl, appearing to study it. "Simone? Are you okay?"

"Me?" Simone glanced up at Chim Chim. "Yeah, sure. I'm fine."

Chim Chim noticed that the sharp, intelligent look in Simone's eyes had been replaced with a dull, unfocused stare.

Simone left the bowl untouched and padded past Chim Chim. "I'm going out to the patio table to take a nap."

"A nap? You've just *had* a nap!" Chim Chim was starting to feel alarmed. "What about breakfast?"

Simone paused, looking back. "Oh. I'm not really hungry." She turned and pushed through the pet door.

Chim Chim raced after her. She found Simone gazing up at the patio table—normally her favorite spot to nap.

"I'm—I'm going to sleep on the sofa," Simone said. She turned and padded away.

Chim Chim studied the marine-print furniture. The sofa and matching chair were definitely a foot shorter than the glass-topped table. But since when could Simone not jump a mere two and a half feet?

Zoe appeared next to her. "This isn't like Simone at all."

"No, it's not. Do you think she's sick?"

"It's possible," Zoe mused. "But more likely, there's something fishy going on here."

"Fishy?" Chim Chim asked. "As in smelly? Or suspicious?"

"*Definitely* suspicious." Zoe frowned. She padded over to the screened window to study the street. "Audrey should be well enough away by now." She rejoined Chim Chim. "Let's do some detective work of our own."

Chim Chim nodded. She stole a look at Simone before she followed Zoe back through the pet door. They padded over to the kitchen cabinet that held the pet supplies.

"You'll have to do the paw-work, Junior. I'm too old to leap onto high counters anymore."

"Oh, yeah. Sure." Chim Chim sprang agilely onto the

imitation-granite countertop and waited for further instructions.

"Isn't that the drawer where Audrey keeps our medicines?" Zoe asked.

"Yep." Chim Chim leaned over and tapped the drawer knob with her paw. "Right here."

"Good. See if you can find anything with Simone's name on it."

Chim Chim felt her jaw drop. "You don't think Audrey's drugging Simone now, too?"

"I don't just *think*," Zoe said. "I am willing to bet a month's worth of canned food that she's doing exactly that."

Chim Chim pried the drawer open a few inches with her paw. She couldn't see much, so she pushed it farther.

"Be careful not to pull it out too much—these drawers can fall out if they're pulled too far."

"Oh—right!" Chim Chim said.

"You're doing fine," Zoe assured her. "What do you see?"

Chim Chim pulled an almost-empty medicine bottle toward the front of the drawer. She pawed it around until she could see its label. She gasped. "This bottle has *my* name on it!" She squinted at the tiny words. "Oh, wait. It's dated five years ago—it must have been from when I was a kitten."

"Yes, Audrey's bad about throwing out expired medicines. Keep looking."

Chim Chim reached deeper into the drawer. All she found were the flea drops Audrey put on the back of their necks and some hairball treats. "Nothing in here." She pawed the door closed and turned to study the counter-top. The basket on the countertop was empty, but behind it was a small white box she hadn't seen before. "Hold on." She nosed the basket out of the way to get a better look. "Bingo!" Chim Chim pressed on the box lightly with a paw, accidentally knocking it over.

"You found a pill bottle?" Zoe asked.

"No. But I found an empty box that says, '*Tranquilta, Oral Suspension, 30mg/mL*.' Below that is a label with Simone's name printed on it. *I knew it!*"

"Oh, my." Zoe remained quiet for a few seconds. "The term *mL* stands for 'milliliter'—which means that Audrey must have bought the liquid version this time. It would be easier to give to us, since she could mix it in with our canned food, and we might not notice."

Chim Chim gasped. "She must have figured out that Simone didn't swallow the first pill—but *how?*"

"I don't know, Junior." Zoe shook her head. "She may have realized Simone wasn't having the effect she was trying to achieve—whatever that could possibly be. But more importantly, *where* is the missing bottle?"

Chim Chim turned to the empty box with a heavy sigh.

Chim Chim lay on the patio table, gazing out at the street. She felt like the wind had completely left her sails—as if she were floating on an endless ocean aboard a tiny raft, with no help in sight. She exhaled slowly. *What do I do now?*

All her life—all five years of it—she'd always had Simone to guide her, to give her good advice, and to call her out on her crap. If she'd been scared, Simone stepped in to take over. When she'd been unsure of the next step, Simone always had a plan. Now, she was completely on her own. Sure—she still had Zoe. But the older cat could no longer do a lot of the physical stuff required in detective work. Plus, last year's petnapping case had taken a toll on Zoe. She didn't leave the house as much now.

Her thoughts were interrupted by the sound of the telephone. *Ring! Ring!* Chim Chim lifted her head from her paws and waited. There was a brief silence, followed by another ring. Definitely a call for Crime Busters! She dashed through the inner pet door, leaping onto the kitchen counter. She pressed the green button on the phone, as she'd seen Simone do countless times. "Hello?" she said nervously. She held her breath as she waited for a reply.

"Chim Chim!" said the high-pitched voice on the other end. "It's Sabrina!"

"Oh." Chim Chim let out her pent-up breath in a rush. "Hi, Sabrina." She allowed herself a smile at the sound of the little Yorkie's voice. "Did you get the items we needed?"

"I couldn't get a glass—but I got a fork *and* a cloth napkin."

"Awesome." Chim Chim could almost imagine Sabrina's proud grin on the other end. "You did a great job." She glanced at the clock on the wall. It was only 1:00 p.m. "I'll be over in ten minutes to pick them up. Meet me at your pet door, okay?"

"I will. Bye, Chim Chim!"

"Bye."

Chim Chim pushed the call-end button and nudged the phone back onto its cradle. She jumped down, pushing through the pet door to the Florida room. She padded over to the patio sofa and studied Simone. The white cat hadn't moved or changed positions since that morning.

"Simone?" She gave her housemate a nudge with her paw. *"Simone?"*

"Yes?" Simone's voice sounded thick, as if her tongue were wrapped in cotton. Her eyes remained closed.

"Sabrina called. She's got the fingerprint evidence for us."

"Okay," Simone said. "That's great." She tucked her tail more tightly under her chin.

"Simone? *Ugh!*"

Chim Chim sighed in exasperation as Simone started to snore. She gave up and padded over to the outer pet door. For the first time in her life, she felt completely and utterly alone. She took a deep breath to steady her nerves. It was time to put on her big-girl pants and get to work.

She pushed through the pet door with a *swoosh! Clang, clang, clang!*

CHAPTER 18
Fangful Encounter

Chim Chim padded across the narrow canal bridge again. It would have given her a sense of *déjà vu*—the feeling that it had all happened before—except that this time, Simone wasn't with her. This time, she was on her own.

She continued down Pine Street, staying close to the grassy lawns. As she neared Sabrina's home, the autumn sun began to warm her black coat. She paused to study the neighboring houses. Satisfied that no one was watching, she padded around the side of Sabrina's house to the backyard. She leaped expertly over the four-foot chain-link fence and landed with a soft thud in the St. Augustine grass.

Chim Chim giggled at the sight of the oak, remembering how Simone had used the tree to cross the fence the day before. But the smile faded rapidly as worry about Simone's condition crept back into her mind. She strode across the concrete patio in a somber mood.

Sabrina poked her head through the pet door as she approached. Chim Chim noticed the little dog wore purple bows at her ears today—Davina must have taken her to the groomer since their last visit.

"Hi, Chim Chim!" Sabrina greeted. "Come on in." She pulled her head back inside.

Chim Chim stepped through the pet door, her mood still gloomy. Even Sabrina's ear-to-ear grin didn't cheer her up.

"Chim Chim," Sabrina said, tilting her head. "What's wrong?" She glanced suddenly at the pet door. "And where's Simone?"

"Simone's not coming today," Chim Chim said. "I—I don't know when she'll be able to leave the house again."

"Not coming?" Sabrina's brow furrowed. "Why?"

"It's my fault. We were so busy trying to get evidence on Dr. Edwards that I didn't notice Audrey was about to medicate Simone, too." The emotions welling up inside of Chim Chim were too strong. Her eyes flooded with tears, and she was completely unable to stop them. "It's all . . . my . . . fault." She began to sob.

"Oh, Chim Chim . . . it's okay." The little Yorkie—no bigger than a tomcat—rushed over and laid a front paw on Chim Chim's shoulder. "It will be fine," Sabrina soothed. Her normally high-pitched voice lowered an octave as she rubbed Chim Chim's back. Surprisingly, it was exactly what Chim Chim needed. Sabrina's touch was warm and comforting, despite her small size. Chim Chim's sobs slowed and soon stopped. She dabbed at her tears with a paw, sniffling as she sought to regain control.

"I'm sorry. I don't know where that came from."

"Oh, it's all right," Sabrina said. "That's what friends are for." She beamed happily.

Chim Chim managed a smile in return. That's *definitely* what friends were for. She took a deep breath to steady herself. "Okay. Now where is this evidence you collected for me?"

"Oh, that—right!" Sabrina scurried over to the large cream-colored sofa and poked a paw under the leather dust flap at the bottom. Pulling out a plastic baggie, she leaned down and grabbed it in her tiny teeth. She carried it over and dropped it at Chim Chim's feet.

Chim Chim pawed at the bag, maneuvering it so she could see its contents. Sure enough, it contained a fork and a burgundy cloth napkin. She smirked. She had *never* seen cloth napkins at their house—Audrey only bought the cheap paper ones.

"Great job, Sabrina. I owe you one for this."

"No problem," the Yorkie said. "It was rather easy, actually." She wagged her short tail. "Oh—but there *is* one thing."

"Yeah? What?"

Sabrina frowned. "I don't know if I should worry, or . . ." She trailed off, scurrying to a cabinet that faced the kitchen island. She nudged the door open with her nose. "I found this while I was rummaging around, looking for a baggie." She stood back to let Chim Chim have a look.

Chim Chim padded over to the cabinet and peered in. She gasped as she saw a small brown pill bottle with familiar writing on the white label. She didn't want to alarm Sabrina, but she had to warn her so her little friend could stay alert.

"What is it?" Sabrina's tiny brows furrowed anxiously.

"Maybe nothing. Has Davina tried to give you anything—like a pill or liquid—with your food?"

Sabrina squinted her eyes as she thought for a second. "No, I don't think so."

"That's good. Really good." Chim Chim held Sabrina's gaze while she spoke. "Listen, this is the same medicine that Audrey used on Zoe and Simone—*Tranquilta*. You want to make sure Davina doesn't give you any, no matter what."

"Oh, my! Definitely not." The little Yorkie shook her head.

Chim Chim's breath drew in sharply. "Oh." Her paw flew to her mouth.

"What?" Sabrina asked. Her eyes widened. "What, Chim Chim?"

"I'll bet *this* was what Dr. Edwards gave Davina at the Halloween party! I'm surprised she hasn't tried to give you some."

"Well, Davina is a pretty smart human," Sabrina said. "She must have looked up the side effects first."

"Thank goodness she did," Chim Chim said. "I wish Audrey would have been that smart." She sighed. "Just keep an eye out. I wouldn't want anything to happen to you."

Sabrina nodded.

Chim Chim gave Sabrina a shy smile. "And thanks for the hug. Really—it meant a lot."

Sabrina giggled. "That's what friends are for, remember?"

"Yeah." Chim Chim nodded. "Yeah, I do. But hey—"

"Yes, Chim Chim?"

"Can we keep it to ourselves?" Chim Chim lowered her voice, even though no one else was in the room. "It would ruin my detective's reputation if word got out that I sank into tears the first time I went out on my own."

"Sure, no problem!" Sabrina grinned, showing her tiny, sharp teeth.

"Thanks, Sabrina. Take care of yourself."

"You, too." Sabrina wagged her tail excitedly. "Bye, Chim Chim."

"Bye."

Chim Chim leaned down and grasped the baggie gently in her jaws. Giving Sabrina a nod, she padded to the pet door and pushed back out into the warm November sunshine.

The half-moon provided sufficient light, but Chim Chim kept to the shadows that night. Her heart thudded in her chest as she padded down block after endless city block. She didn't know how Simone always seemed so confident about strolling through Valencia Springs at night. Chim Chim was a nervous wreck!

She couldn't hum any happy tunes—a practice that helped calm her nerves—because of the bag she carried gently in her jaws. Earlier, she had swapped out Sabrina's evidence from the plastic bag to a brown paper one she found in Audrey's kitchen drawer. She'd learned from Simone that plastic could sweat, and she didn't want Dr. Edwards's fingerprints to be destroyed. Now that *she* was in charge, she couldn't afford any mistakes.

Chim Chim concentrated instead on her breathing. She mentally counted 1-2-3-4 with each inward breath, then 1-2-3-4 with each exhale. It seemed to help. She soon reached the end of the residential district and continued toward downtown. The red metal stop signs were replaced with traffic lights that brightened the intersections with green, then yellow, and finally red. Red seemed to be a universal human color that meant "stop."

She paused as she neared the last block before the police station. She had never met this Caleb, and he wasn't expecting her. But she hadn't known the number to Officer Pearson's desk, so she was unable to contact Caleb by phone.

She padded up to the plate glass windows in front of the police station and peered in. The waiting area was empty, with not a human in sight. A service counter topped with glass spanned the back of the room. She figured it was bulletproof glass, like at the bank—police department employees had to be careful. A door behind the counter opened suddenly, and a man walked through, carrying a steaming coffee mug. Chim Chim thought he looked pleasant, but she scurried off. She didn't want to press her luck.

Chim Chim remembered Simone saying that Caleb had a potty break around 8:00 p.m. when he worked the night shift. Simone had also mentioned an alley in back where she usually waited for him. So Chim Chim decided to check it out.

She continued past the main entrance and around the side of the building. Padding a few feet down the paved alleyway, she stopped at a group of trash cans near the back door of the precinct. A light over the door illuminated a few feet of the dark alley, but the trash cans remained in the shadows.

Chim Chim laid the paper bag on the ground next to her, hoping she wouldn't have long to wait. She wasn't sure what time it was, but she knew it was past closing time for many of the businesses downtown. Valencia Springs was small enough to have quiet streets at night, unlike the traffic problems in big cities. She was thankful for that.

An hour passed slowly, and she didn't realize she'd fallen into a light sleep until the back door of the precinct flew open. She jerked awake with a start.

"There you go, boy. Don't wander off," said a kindly human voice.

A fearsome red-and-black German shepherd trotted out. He nosed about, stopping at a cement block to lift his leg and mark it with his scent. He nosed around a little more, then stopped, frozen in place. Chim Chim could see the hackles on his neck and back lift in the dim light. A warning growl rose from deep within his throat, causing the blood in Chim Chim's veins to turn to ice.

"Who's there?" he growled. "I can't see you, but the smell of cat is everywhere."

Chim Chim gulped as every hair on her body stood up. She wished she could melt into the ground and disappear! "Um . . ." she broke off, her voice shaky. "My name is Chim Chim. I'm Simone's housemate. I'm . . . I'm . . . with Crime Busters," she sputtered. The fear gripped her throat like a vise, making the words hard to speak.

Caleb's stance relaxed, his hackles lowering. He laughed. "Chim Chim?" He snorted. "Well, why didn't you *say* so?" His growl had disappeared, and his tail gave a wag as he strode over to join her.

Chim Chim had forgotten to breathe. She gulped a fresh breath of air as he approached, willing her fur to lay flat.

Caleb stopped a few inches away, grinning to reveal a sharp set of pearly-white teeth. He sniffed the air again. "Yeah, I should have guessed—you have that same faint scent of apples that Simone always has."

Chim Chim concentrated on keeping her fur flat, reminding herself that this dog was a friend of Simone's—and he wouldn't hurt his friend's dearest housemate. "Air freshener," she said timidly. "Our owner uses those air freshener devices that you plug into the wall." She paused. "Apple spice is her favorite."

"Oh." Caleb nodded. "Well, I've heard a lot about you, Chim Chim," he said in his raspy voice. "Sorry to alarm you. I don't get too many visitors at night."

"It's okay," Chim Chim said. She gave a shy smile as her composure slowly returned. "I'm sorry, too. I didn't know the number to your handler's—to Detective Pearson's—desk, so I had to come see you in person."

"Come see me," Caleb repeated. His brow suddenly furrowed. "Where's Simone?"

Chim Chim swallowed hard. "Well, that's the problem. Simone's been drugged—I mean, medicated—by our owner. It's all thanks to Audrey's beady-eyed boyfriend!" She felt the burn of anger deep within her stomach.

"You mean Neal?" Caleb growled. "Simone told me about him. *Evil man.*" He bared his teeth as he emphasized the last words. "I hate that this happened to her."

Chim Chim sighed. "Yeah. Me, too." She looked down at her paws, suddenly remembering the bag she'd brought. "Oh—that's why I'm here. I have the fingerprint evidence from Dr. Edwards you asked for." She pushed the bag toward Caleb with her paw.

"Excellent," Caleb said. He sniffed the bag briefly. "You did good, kid. Simone would be proud of you."

"Thanks." Chim Chim gave a grim smile. She would rather Simone be there with her.

"I'm going to process these prints, then run them through the federal database," Caleb said. "I'll bet our Dr. Edwards is hiding something—and I plan to find it."

"I sure hope so."

"I'll call as soon as I'm done," Caleb said. "I'll use the secret ring, so be ready to answer."

"I will," Chim Chim promised. She turned to go.

"And hey, kid—"

"Yes?"

Caleb's dark eyes were sympathetic. "It's going to be okay—I've got your back."

Chim Chim nodded. She turned and padded back down the dark alley.

CHAPTER 19
Frankenstein Monster

Chim Chim paced the kitchen floor. She'd waited all morning for Caleb's call, but the phone remained silent. She peeked around the corner into the living room, where Simone lay curled on the couch. Her housemate remained in a stupor, either sleeping or walking about in a daze. Simone neither ate, nor spoke. And to be honest, Chim Chim was terrified—terrified that she would lose Simone, terrified that she'd end up all alone once Zoe was gone. Zoe was elderly, so her years left with them were limited.

She and Zoe had tried to find the bottle of liquid Tranquilta, but Audrey was keeping it well hidden. Chim Chim could only assume that Neal must have become suspicious when the other bottles had gone missing and advised Audrey to hide it. How long would it be before Chim Chim herself fell victim to Neal's hostile anti-cat takeover?

She sighed, resuming her pacing of the floor. Pacing helped distract her from worrying, and that usually helped her to think. Suddenly the shrill ring of the phone sounded in the silent house. Chim Chim leaped upon the counter and waited, listening. The phone rang twice, then stopped. She pushed it from its cradle, hovering over the device with a ready paw. When it began to ring again, she quickly jabbed at the green button. "Hello?"

"Chim Chim," came the raspy reply. "It's Caleb."

"Hi, Caleb," she said nervously.

"Listen, kid," Caleb began. Chim Chim could hear excitement in his voice. "Have I got some news for you!"

"Yeah?" Chim Chim felt her heartbeat quicken.

"Yeah. I ran the prints you brought me through the federal database, and I came up with a 100-percent match—but not to Dr. Ryan Edwards."

"Excuse me?" Chim Chim frowned, puzzled. The prints *had* to belong to Dr. Edwards—Sabrina saw him using the fork and napkin herself! "Then who did they belong to?"

"Edwards's prints match up with a veterinarian in Georgia named Michael Frazier. Ring a bell?"

"Um . . . no," Chim Chim said. "Or maybe? I'm not sure."

"Michael Frazier is the vet who made all the headlines as 'Dr. Death' in Sandy Springs, Georgia," Caleb said. "He was arrested for prescribing veterinary drugs that hadn't been approved by the FDA, which led to multiple pet deaths. They tried to bust the company that distributed them, but if I remember correctly, the FDA wasn't able to prove they had sold them to Frazier—something to do with evidence that wasn't handled correctly."

"Oh, yeah." Chim Chim began to nod. "I think I remember Simone mentioning Dr. Death. But why would their prints match? Unless—oh, my gosh—it's the *same* guy!"

"Apparently so," Caleb agreed. "His nose looks a little different, and he's wearing glasses in the mug shot. But it's definitely him. I can't believe he got out of jail so quickly—or that he was able to forge a new identity and fake medical license."

"Me, either." Chim Chim shook her head in amazement. "So, what do we do now?"

"Well, kid . . ." Caleb trailed off with a sigh. "I hate to say it, but after law enforcement bungled the last investigation—with the evidence and all—we need to make double-sure that Dr. Edwards gets put away for good this time."

"I'm with you on that."

"So I think we need *more* than his fingerprints."

"More?" Chim Chim swallowed hard. A rock formed in the pit of her stomach as she thought she knew the direction this conversation was going. *Why do I always get pulled into schemes that involve danger?* "What do you propose?"

"I have an idea . . . but if you're too afraid, you don't have to agree to it."

"Go ahead."

"John scheduled me for my annual exam and shots this Friday—that's only three days away. If I can create a distraction while I'm there, I can disable Dr. Edwards's alarm system and unlock a window in my exam room. The clinic isn't open for business this weekend. That would give you Saturday and Sunday to sneak in and search for evidence."

"*Me?*" Chim Chim squeaked.

"I know," Caleb said. "I'm asking a lot—I'm sorry. Can your other housemate go with you?"

"Zoe? No, she's too old. With her arthritis, she'd never be able to make it across town on foot."

"You're right," Caleb agreed. "Never mind. I'm sorry I even suggested something so dangerous."

Chim Chim was silent for a moment. Her friends' lives hung in the balance now. She couldn't just think of herself.

"Are you still there, kid?"

"Yeah." Chim Chim gave a deep sigh. "I'll do it." She suddenly felt very heavy, as if gravity had tripled, and she could barely lift her limbs. "But it will have to be on Sunday. Audrey sleeps late, so I'll be able to sneak out of the house."

"Sunday it is, then," Caleb agreed. "Look—if there's any way I can get over there to help, I will, all right? I promise."

"Sure." Chim Chim gave a grim smile, though Caleb couldn't see it.

"I'll call on Friday to confirm that I did my part," Caleb said. "If anything goes wrong, we'll scrap the plan and come up with something else." He paused. "We can do this. It will be okay."

"I know," Chim Chim said, sounding more convinced than she felt. "Thanks, Caleb."

"No problem, kid. I'll talk to you then. Goodbye."

"Bye." Chim Chim's paw shook as she reached to click the red button on the phone. She was terrified again. But this time, it wasn't for Simone—it was for herself.

"Getting in over your head, Junior?" Zoe asked softly from behind her.

Chim Chim turned to see her elderly housemate's somber expression. "I don't know what I just agreed to," she said, her voice trembling. "It's either the second-bravest thing I'm ever going to do, or it will be the end of my short life on this planet."

Zoe cocked her head. "The first-bravest thing being when you faced the petnappers?"

Chim Chim nodded.

"Well, it seems to me that you must have a deep well of courage, Junior. I can't say I would've stood against those awful men last year—but neither would I be drawn into another dangerous plot this time around."

Chim Chim gave a halfhearted laugh. "Hmm . . . yeah."

"What I *can* suggest," Zoe said, "is that you give this some deep thought. Only you can say what is right for you. Only *you* can decide if it's worth the risk. Listen to that voice of wisdom deep inside. It will tell you what to do—and it's rarely ever wrong."

Chim Chim nodded again. "I guess you're right."

Zoe laid a paw on her shoulder. "It will be okay, kid, whatever you decide." She smiled and padded away, leaving Chim Chim alone with her thoughts.

Why was everyone saying that these days? She had a bad feeling that this weekend may turn out to be quite the opposite.

CHAPTER 20

Dr. Jekyll and Miss (Hide!)

Sunday morning, Chim Chim rose early. She needed to leave the house unseen, and the best way to do that was to sneak out while Audrey and her housemates were sleeping. She'd been awake for hours, anyway. Her mind was too anxious to allow sleep.

The Sunday morning traffic was light, so Chim Chim trotted safely across quiet streets toward the northeast side of town. The air had turned cooler overnight, making travel quite comfortable. She tried not to think about the task ahead of her—if her heart pounded any harder, she feared it might burst through her ribcage. Instead, she hummed softly to distract her mind.

Twenty minutes later, she approached Dr. Edwards's sprawling new clinic on the corner of Spaulding and Orange Valley Road. She paused underneath a boxwood hedge that bordered the empty parking lot. Her nose wrinkled in distaste as she studied the modern facility. The building's exterior was tan stucco, accented with beautiful oak beams and lots of high glass windows. Expensive for sure.

Caleb had called on Friday to confirm that he'd successfully unlocked the window in Exam Room 3—the room used for large dogs. He hadn't been able to turn off the alarm system, though. So he'd advised her to search quickly and get far away from there before the police arrived.

"Let's do this," Chim Chim whispered to herself. "One paw before the other." She padded across the silent parking lot and stepped onto the cool concrete of the sidewalk. She then followed the sidewalk around the northern side of the building, where she knew the exam rooms stood. She mentally counted the windows. Each exam room had a window, and the first room was for cats. The second room was for small dogs. So that made the third window her lucky one—or so she hoped. She stepped off into the damp morning grass. *Blah!* She hated the feel of damp paws.

Chim Chim approached the window warily. She glanced both ways, then bunched her leg muscles and sprang up onto the window's narrow ledge. Leaning down, she wedged her front paws under the window sill and gave it an upward tug. The window rose easily from its sill, allowing her to peer into the dimly lit room inside. She took a deep breath to calm her jittery nerves. Then she jumped down and padded across the tiled floor. She looked back, realizing she had left wet paw prints on the tiles. *Oops.*

She grimaced as she passed the stainless steel exam table. Definitely not her favorite place! She paused, studying the scale and veterinary supplies on the nearby counter. She doubted there would be any evidence there, so she continued into the dark hallway. Glancing to the left, Chim Chim could see the reception desk and customer waiting area beyond Exam Rooms 1 and 2. To her right was the room used for surgery, with the lab across from it. A closed door at the end of the hall drew her attention.

Chim Chim padded slowly toward the room at the end, growing more anxious with each paw step. The name plate on the door read, "Dr. Edwards," so she knew it must be the vet's office. It was also the most likely place to find damaging evidence. Rising on her back feet, she stretched, grasping the door knob with both front paws. She squeezed, turning it to the left. The knob clicked and the door opened inward, causing Chim Chim to lose her balance.

Suddenly, a shrill voice sounded behind her. "Pretty bird!" Chim Chim jerked, her heart racing, as a white feathered form flew into the first exam room. She shook her head. It was only the clinic's star cockatiel, Figaro. *Stay calm,* she reminded herself. She took a deep breath and entered the room.

Her feline gaze adjusted quickly to the darkness inside. Dr. Edwards kept the charcoal-gray blinds on his windows closed, so no light was able to enter. But an illuminated clock next to his desk showed that it was 8:00—still too early for Audrey to notice she was missing.

Chim Chim leaped onto Dr. Edwards's massive walnut desk. She smirked, hoping her paws were still damp. She would love to see his meltdown when he saw paw prints all over his desk Monday morning! Padding to the edge, she leaned over and pawed open the drawer to the right of his desk chair. Rifling through its contents, she found nothing out of the ordinary: a spare stethoscope, note-pads, and pens. She pulled open the drawer on the left side of the desk and found a mesh container with paper clips, some sticky notes, and a stapler—nothing damaging to his reputation.

She gathered her leg muscles and jumped onto the credenza—a fancy name for a desk with cabinets above it—behind Dr. Edwards's walnut desk. The credenza had shallow drawers on either side, with two deeper drawers underneath. She tugged on the shallow drawer to the left with a forepaw, but it was locked. She padded over to the drawers on the right—also locked. *Hmm . . . did the dear doc have something to hide?*

Chim Chim leaped back to the walnut desk and pawed open the drawer that contained the paper clips. Pushing the lid off the black mesh container with her nose, she grabbed a shiny silver paper clip in her teeth and sprang across to the credenza. Holding the clip between her teeth, she pulled on it with her front paws until she had straightened one end. Then she inserted the straight end into the lock of the left-side drawer, just like Simone had taught her. *Simone!* Her breath drew in sharply as a familiar rock settled in her stomach. No—she couldn't think about Simone right now. She needed to concentrate on the task at hand.

Chim Chim jiggled the paper clip around until she heard a *click!* Then she pulled it out with her teeth and jerked open the drawer. *Let's see what you're hiding, Dr. Frankenstein!* She frowned, finding only a stack of medical equipment brochures. But unlocking the top drawer had also freed up the deep one below it. Pulling the deep drawer open with a paw, Chim Chim discovered a handful of file folders that were turned *backwards*. Definitely suspicious!

She gave a snort as she pulled out the first of the file folders and laid it flat on the credenza's surface. Her brows knit together as she read the label. It had what sounded like a drug name, *Formeezia,* next to a date. Beneath that was the name *Bruster Pharmaceutical Company.* Very puzzling, indeed. She opened the folder and looked inside. It contained several papers that were printed with the Bruster Pharmaceutical logo. "Hmm." She knew a "pharmaceutical" was a medical drug, so a pharmaceutical *company* would most likely manufacture and sell medicines. She pulled the other folders out, one at a time, and studied the dates on them. There were five of them in all. The first three file folders were dated nine years ago, but the last two were labeled with the current year—and the name on the very last folder made her gasp. *Tranquilta!*

She hurriedly pushed the other folders aside and opened the Tranquilta folder. As she rifled through its contents, she stopped, her paw in midair. She squinted at a piece of paper addressed to Dr. Edwards. It was a letter written by the president of Bruster, dated nine months ago. She scanned through the body of the letter, gasping as she read the final paragraph.

Ryan, I want to congratulate you personally on your return to veterinary practice. May our mutual business arrangement be as beneficial now as it was during your time in Georgia. (Please see attached check.) Don't hesitate to reach me if you need anything.

Best regards,
Phil

This letter was exactly what she needed! The illegal drugs that Dr. Edwards—a.k.a. "Doctor Death"—had prescribed in Georgia must have come from Bruster Pharmaceuticals. There was no check attached, so Chim Chim assumed the doc had cashed it. She studied the logo at the top of the page, drawing her breath in sharply again.

Bruster Pharmaceutical Company
A Division of Divinity Laboratories, Inc.

She knew it! She knew there was something fishy about this whole business. Divinity Labs was the company from Jacksonville that she and Simone had exposed last year for their illegal activities.

Chim Chim was pulled from her thoughts as she heard a click, followed by the slam of a door and a series of beeps as someone disarmed the alarm. *Oh, no!* Her heart lurched into her throat as she realized she was no longer alone in the clinic. She jumped down hastily and darted under the walnut desk.

Heavy footsteps grew louder as a human entered the hallway. Chim Chim peered out from under the desk, her breath drawing in sharply as the blood froze in her veins. *Dr Edwards!!* How had he gotten here so quickly?

The tall veterinarian's face bore a look of annoyance as he strode down the hall, ducking his head into each room as he passed. "Figaro!" he called. "Figaro! Where are you, you crazy bird?"

Chim Chim remembered hearing that Figaro was quite skilled at opening his cage door—and at setting off the security alarm! She hadn't heard an alarm go off, so the Doc must have it set to silent mode.

Dr. Edwards continued toward her, pausing in front of the open door to his office. "What the—" he muttered angrily, pushing the door fully inward. He flicked on the light switch, his eyes narrowing as he discovered the file folders strewn across the credenza. He turned suddenly, looking back down the silent hallway. "Who's there?" he demanded. "I know *someone's* in here—that dumb bird couldn't do this." Greeted with only silence, he turned back to the chaos in his office. He approached his desk in two quick strides.

As he rounded the corner, Chim Chim shot out from under the desk, flying down the hallway as fast as her sleek legs could carry her.

"Why—you little *troublemaker!*"

Chim Chim heard the sound of fast, heavy footsteps behind her as she darted back into Exam Room 3. Her breath came in ragged gasps as she bolted toward the open window. But her short cat legs were no match for Dr. Edwards's large human stride. He dashed around the steel exam table, cutting her off from the window—and her only means of escape.

"You're a smart little thing," Dr. Edwards said, his eyes glittering. "Too smart for your own good. What did you think you were going to find in there?"

He lunged and grabbed Chim Chim by the scruff of her neck. Every muscle froze, then went limp, as her heart threatened to stop right then and there. He lifted her easily, his cruel fingers squeezing her delicate skin, and strode down the hall. "Well, they don't call me 'Dr. Death' for nothing."

Another chill went through Chim Chim at his words. It couldn't end like this! She was supposed to *save* everybody from the bad guy—not become another of his victims!

Dr. Edwards opened the door to the lab and stomped over to a row of metal cages. Unhooking the latch on one of them, he thrust Chim Chim inside and slammed the cage door. "Stay put for a minute." He shuffled over to a locked medicine cabinet. Pulling a set of keys from his pocket, he unlocked the cabinet and pulled out a small glass bottle. He relocked the cabinet and carried the bottle to a counter nearby, pulling out the drawer underneath.

Chim Chim's eyes grew large as Dr. Edwards grabbed a syringe from the drawer and removed its paper packaging.

Holding the bottle upside down, he inserted the needle end of the syringe and drew a large amount of fluid into its hollow body.

Dr. Edwards turned to her, his eyes filled with the twisted gleam of hate. Chim Chim *knew* her heart had surely stopped as he approached and reopened the cage door. Her mind whirled as she tried to come up with a plan of escape. She scooted toward the back of the cage, but he reached in and grabbed her easily by her scruff. Striding down the hall, he carried her back into Exam Room 3 and placed her upon the cold steel exam table. He looked into her eyes as he held her down with one hand.

"Say good-bye, my little friend. I'm sure you've guessed by now that I have no great love for animals—only for making money. And I can't let you jeopardize that."

He laughed then, a sound so chilling that Chim Chim forgot to breathe. Why had she thought she could do this on her own? Now she had failed miserably—she'd failed Simone, she'd failed Zoe . . . she had failed them all. Dr. Edwards depressed the tip of the syringe to expel any air bubbles. It would all be over soon.

At the thought of Simone, a small ball grew in the pit of her stomach—a tiny ball of fire that expanded, filling every cell of her being with adrenaline and the heat of anger. NO—*it is* not *going to end like this! He is not getting away with this!* She breathed in deeply and let the anger fill her lungs.

As the doctor used the fingers of his free hand to part the fur on her right foreleg, she lunged, sinking her tiny, sharp teeth into his skin.

"*YEOW!!*" He jerked his hand back, dropping the syringe and giving her the valuable seconds she needed. She jumped down and dashed toward the window, bunching her rear leg muscles for the leap to safety. Suddenly, a large shape sailed over her head. She fell back on her haunches, stunned, as a rush of air ruffled her fur. A deep, frenzied growl reached her ears.

She turned to see the red-and-black body of a German shepherd as it drove Dr. Edwards into a corner. The doctor desperately shielded his face with his hands as the dog lunged repeatedly. The canine's razor-sharp teeth connected with the denim of Dr. Edwards's blue jeans, making jagged tears. *Caleb!* But how had he gotten here?

A loud commotion quickly drowned out Caleb's vicious growl. Chim Chim heard a loud slam, followed by multiple heavy footsteps. She backed up against the wall below the window, uncertain whether she should remain or escape.

A middle-aged man with slightly-graying hair entered the room, his gun drawn. "Caleb! There you are. Back off, boy! Back off—I've got this."

Caleb—trained to obey his handler—released his bite and backed away from his prey. The German shepherd trotted over to Chim Chim, giving her a wink before turning to watch the humans.

John Pearson kept his eyes and gun locked on Dr. Edwards. "Now don't you move a muscle, son. You're under arrest." More humans entered the room, these in police uniforms, with guns also drawn. John turned to them. "He's all yours, boys." He kept his gun aimed at

Dr. Edwards until the doctor was safely in handcuffs. Then he holstered it and strode over, giving Caleb a warm rub and a scratch behind the ears. "Well done, boy! Good job." He turned to study Chim Chim with kind blue eyes. "Friend of yours?" he asked Caleb. He glanced over at the syringe on the floor. "Looks like you got here in the nick of time."

Nick of time was right! Chim Chim tried to calm her breathing as John reached down and picked her up. He held her close to his chest and gently stroked the fur along her neck and back. She relaxed a little, allowing herself to enjoy his kind touch—so different from the painful bite of Dr. Edwards's cold fingers. She guessed humans could be as different as night from day, just as animals could.

Her heartbeat slowed its rapid pace as John placed her gently back onto the floor. He followed the uniformed officers as they led the handcuffed Dr. Edwards out of the room. Chim Chim turned to Caleb. "How did you know I was in trouble? And *how* did you get the police here?"

Caleb grinned, his sharp teeth no longer menacing. "Well, John and I stopped by the station this morning—so John could finish up some paperwork. You must have entered the clinic about the same time, because the monitoring company called to report a triggered alarm. A few seconds later, a call came in from Dr. Edwards, telling us to disregard the alarm. He said *he* had set it off accidentally." Caleb narrowed his eyes. "I knew something didn't sound right—call it a dog's 'inner wisdom.'"

Chim Chim smiled. She was hearing that phrase a lot these days.

"Dr. Edwards was already under John's suspicion, thanks to me," Caleb continued. "I'd laid the FBI fingerprint report—along with my recent vaccination bill from Dr. Edwards—out on Friday for John to find. It took him no time to put 'two and two' together." He chuckled. "John's pretty smart."

"I'd say! So he knew to drive you over here just now?" Chim Chim asked, amazed.

Caleb snorted. "No, not exactly. . . You see, I'm no longer on active patrol, which means I don't have to be kenneled in the backseat anymore. So on our way home from the station, I, uh . . . hit the window button and jumped out at the red light. It took John completely by surprise—I've *never* acted up, in all our seven years together. We were only a couple of blocks away, so I raced on over, knowing he would follow." Caleb shrugged. "He must have called for backup when I led him here."

Chim Chim exhaled slowly. Her eyes filled with tears as she realized how close to death she had come. "Thank you, Caleb. I might not have made it, if it weren't for you. I—I don't even know how to repay you." A tear rolled silently down her furry cheek.

Caleb laid his large forepaw gently on her shoulder. "It's all right, kid—I'd have done it for anyone. But now *you . . . you're* the true hero around here."

She looked up into his brown eyes and sniffled. "Really?"

"Heck, yeah! I don't know too many *dogs* who would

have risked their lives the way you did—let alone a five-pound cat!" He laughed. "Simone will be proud of you."

Chim Chim felt anxious again. "Do you think she'll be okay?"

"She'll be fine, kiddo—just watch. Once these humans learn the truth about Dr. Edwards, they'll question *all* of his medical advice—including the use of Tranquilta. I'm sure all the city's pets will soon be back to normal."

Chim Chim nodded, dabbing at her eyes with a paw. She hoped he was right. She could use some "normal" about now.

She followed Caleb down the silent hallway toward freedom.

Epilogue

Simone opened her eyes slowly. The morning light filtering through the blinds was a shock to her senses. She realized she was curled against Audrey's pillow. The bed covers had been pulled up underneath her, neat as a pin. As her weary eyes began to make sense of the hazy blurs around her, she focused on the anxious face of Chim Chim close by. Her little buddy's brows were drawn together and her mouth was turned down in a frown.

Zoe lay at the foot of Audrey's bed like a great sphinx, her regal head held high and her front paws outstretched. Her steely gaze watched the doorway.

"Simone!" Chim Chim practically shrieked as Simone refocused her gaze on her youngest housemate. "You're awake!"

"So I am," Simone said with a smile.

Zoe rose and padded closer to Simone. "Welcome back," she said warmly.

"Thanks." Simone gave her forelegs a good stretch, then her back ones. She tried to rise to a sitting position, but her leg muscles felt weak. She collapsed against the pillow with a sigh. *What in the world?* She looked at Zoe and Chim Chim questioningly.

"You'd better take it slow until you get some food in you," Zoe suggested. "You've been out of it for a while."

"Out of it?" Simone repeated, her voice a hoarse whisper. She glanced around at the familiar furnishings in Audrey's room. Nothing seemed different. "What happened? Have I been unconscious?"

"No, but—" Zoe began.

"Audrey went completely off her rocker!" Chim Chim exclaimed. "She started drugging *you*, too!"

"With Tranquilta?" Simone gasped. "But how? She never tried to give me any more pills—not after her first attempt."

"It seems our dear Dr. Edwards prescribed you the liquid version," Zoe said. "Audrey probably sneaked it in with your wet food, and none of us realized it." The elderly cat shook her head.

"Unbe-*liev*-able," Simone said slowly, stressing the middle syllable. "How long was I . . . under its influence?"

"A little over a week," Zoe said. "You never vomited like I did, but you stayed in a daze. You barely ate, and all you did was sleep. We couldn't find the medicine bottle, so Audrey must have continued medicating you until Dr. Edwards's arrest made the news."

"It was terrible, absolutely terrible," Chim Chim said. "But you don't have to worry ever again—I took care of it."

"You," Simone said, peering down her nose at her youngest housemate. "*You* took care of it?"

"Oh, yes indeed," Zoe said, nodding. "You should be very proud of Junior here." She beamed, giving Chim Chim a pat on the shoulder. "Not only did she wrap up the case all by herself, but she made sure Dr. Edwards was put behind bars for good."

Simone pressed a paw to her forehead—her brain must still be foggy from the meds! "Did you say *Chim Chim* solved the case? All by herself?"

Chim Chim shrugged. The insides of her ears turned pink. "Well, not *all* by myself—Caleb helped."

Simone willed her lungs to breathe in and out very slowly. She needed a minute for all of this to register, to sink in.

At that moment Audrey burst in, carrying a plate of food and a small bowl on a wooden bed tray. The savory smell of fish made Simone's nostrils flare. "Good morning, precious girl!" Audrey greeted. "I brought your favorite meal—slightly warmed salmon—and some special treats, too." Audrey gave a sheepish smile as she set the tray on the bed.

"It's your favorite salmon—the kind that comes in the foil packs!" Chim Chim said excitedly.

Audrey laughed, studying Chim Chim. "If I didn't know better, I'd think you just told her what was on the menu."

Simone gave Chim Chim a wink. "*We'll* never tell."

"Nope."

Simone sat up slowly and leaned over the warm plate.

She gave it a sniff, then a nibble. "Mmm . . . my favorite."

"I told you!" Chim Chim exclaimed.

"Go ahead, baby," Audrey urged. "You deserve it after what I put you through—what I put *all* of you through." Her smile suddenly wilted. "I can't believe I let my feelings for another person cloud my own judgment. I am so, so sorry. I promise this will *never* happen again—in fact, I don't care if I ever *date* again!" Her eyes filled with tears as she gave them each a warm rub on their heads.

"Not sorry enough to let the rest of us in on that salmon, I see," Chim Chim said, arching a brow.

Simone and Zoe chuckled.

"So Neal is gone, too?" Simone whispered, her eyes widening. "This day keeps getting better and better."

Chim Chim nodded as Audrey hurried out of the room.

Simone could hear sniffling as their owner disappeared down the hall. She smiled, shaking her head. "Come share in the spoils, my friends." She scooted over to make more room. She noticed Chim Chim didn't need to be told twice—her little buddy ate as if it were the last fish on earth!

After breakfast and a quick cleanup, Simone retired to the patio sofa with Chim Chim and Zoe. "So, tell me *all* about it." She listened intently as Chim Chim recounted the details of finding out that Dr. Edwards was the disgraced "Dr. Death" from Sandy Springs. Simone gasped. "I *knew* there was something fishy about that guy! No pun intended."

"That's what I told you all along," Chim said, rolling her

eyes. She next described the frightful moments at Dr. Edwards's office.

Simone noticed that her little buddy trembled as she retold the story. She placed a front paw on Chim Chim's. "He can't hurt you—or *any* of us—ever again."

Chim Chim nodded, giving her a shy smile.

Simone leaned back against the sofa pillows. The smile on her face was so big it hurt. "I'm so proud of you, Chim Chim!" Her eyes filled with tears as she studied her youngest housemate. She realized now that Chim Chim had grown up—she didn't know why she hadn't seen it before. At five years of age, Chim Chim hadn't just risen to a dangerous challenge; she had followed through—despite the risk to her life—and rid the world of one *major* bad guy.

"I'm proud of you, too, Junior," Zoe said.

Chim Chim puffed up like a proud peacock.

Let her, Simone thought. *She's earned it.* "So, no one's told me how Audrey discovered the truth about Neal." She arched an eyebrow.

Chim Chim grinned. "I thought about leaving Neal's arrest record out for her to find, but we didn't need her wondering how it got there. So instead, I figured out how to turn off the lock screen on Neal's phone. Then I left it in the hallway for her to find, with his text messages from Dr. Edwards pulled up." Chim Chim covered a giggle with her paw. "Boy, was she mad! Her face turned beet red."

"Yeah, she called his office right away," Zoe said excitedly. "There was a lot of yelling on her end, and then she broke up with him."

"And took a hammer to his cell phone!" Chim Chim squealed, dissolving into laughter.

Simone couldn't help but join in. "Either way, we're finally rid of that beady-eyed human. And it sounds like Audrey will be a lot more careful about whom she dates in the future."

"Amen to that," Chim Chim said.

"Amen indeed." Simone gave her pals a huge grin.

Zoe's expression grew serious. "I sure hope the humans in Valencia Springs will learn a lesson from all of this."

"That may take a while," Simone said with a sigh. "Humans can be stubborn."

Zoe nodded. "*Yes*, they can."

"That's okay—Crime Busters will be here to save the day!" Chim Chim declared. Then she gave a deep, fishy belch.

Acknowledgments

First, I would like to thank God for allowing me to realize this dream!

Thanks to all my friends and family who supported me by buying the first Crime Busters book. And thanks to those I don't know who purchased the book—you are friends I have yet to meet. I hope you continue to enjoy Chim Chim and Simone's story.

Thanks to my jefe, John Cruz, for making me wonder what my cats *really* did while I was away at work . . . (Could they be leading secret lives?) I would also like to thank Troy, Scarlett, Chrissy, Stosh, Antigone, Martha, Randy, Frances, and Aunt Diane. Your love and support mean the world to me. (Extra thanks to Scarlett for her amazing artwork!) Much gratitude to Elizabeth Troutman Jordan for being my "first reader" and helping me catch those plot flaws!

Thanks to my writer's group members who have supported me: Billie-Fae Gill, Nancy Keckeisen, Erin Osetek, Charles Ballard, and Jean Moore. Thanks to my "family" at Tabor Presbyterian Church. (Miss Chrissie, you're the best!) Thanks to Michelle Mahaffey of Tybrisa Books and Caitlynne Garland of Dog-Eared Books for your support of local authors.

I would also like to thank friend and fellow writer Jack Kost, for introducing me to the "storyboard" plotting technique. It made writing my second book a hundred times easier! And thanks to dearly departed mystery writer Phyllis A. Whitney. Her book, *Guide to Fiction Writing*, taught me how to be an organized writer.

Heartfelt thanks to Laree and the staff at Electric Moon Publishing for your patience and guidance during the publication of both books. You guys are beyond awesome! Many thanks to Cody Rayn for his exceptional cover art for both books.

And finally, I would like to thank the following people for their help with my research for this novel: Ms. Tanya Pallotta, CLPE; Deputy Jason Shoemaker of the Iredell County Sheriff's Office; Lt. Gary Simpson, Deputy Ben Hardy (& Tito!), Deputy Michael Hicks, and members of the Iredell County Sheriff's Office K-9 Unit; and last, but not at all least, Doctor Robin Brock and Patrick of Farmland Veterinary Clinic. I couldn't have done it without all of you!

About Kiki Houser

Kimberly "Kiki" Houser has tried her hand at everything under the sun: secretary, waitress, video arcade host, preschool teacher, and pet kennel attendant. But she always returns to what she loves most: the *story*, in all its many forms.

Raised in scenic West Virginia and sunny central Florida, Kiki now resides in the Piedmont region of North Carolina with her husband and four children—three of which have whiskers! She spends her time writing children's books, volunteering at school book fairs, and helping conservation groups. *The Alligator Alibi*, the first book in Kiki's feline *Crime Busters, Inc.* series, received two Purple Dragonfly Awards for excellence in children's literature.

Made in the USA
Columbia, SC
08 July 2022